MORE THAN FRIENDS

Kelsey was stunned when Shawn asked, "Would you like to go to homecoming with me?"

"Homecoming?" she asked. That was the last thing she had expected him to say.

"I know you don't date," Shawn continued tentatively. "I thought we could go as friends."

"Friends." Once she got over her initial surprise, Kelsey realized the idea had possibilities. Shawn Horton was a nice person, his great looks aside. And he really sounded sincere about wanting her company at the dance.

"So what do you think? Why don't we go as two friends who couldn't find dates?"

His offer was tempting, and if she wanted to go with Shawn, Kelsey knew she should say yes before he changed his mind.

Bantam Sweet Dreams Romances
Ask your bookseller for the books you have missed

More Than Friends

Janice Boies

BANTAM BOOKS
TORONTO • NEW YORK • LONDON • SYDNEY • AUCKLAND

RL 6, IL age 11 and up

MORE THAN FRIENDS
A Bantam Book / May 1987

Cover photo by Pat Hill

ISBN 0-553-26482-6

Published simultaneously in the United States and Canada

PRINTED IN THE UNITED STATES OF AMERICA

O   0 9 8 7 6 5 4 3 2 1

More Than Friends

Chapter One

Kelsey Kramer dropped her books on the kitchen table. It was only the third week of school, and already she had a chemistry quiz the next day. Trying to forget about her homework for a while, she grabbed an apple from the fruit basket on the counter and started toward the family room. A message on the notepad by the phone made her pause. It was in her mom's handwriting.

> Had to help Dad at the club!
> Casserole in fridge. Please
> put in oven at 4:30.

So, her mom had to help at one of the two health clubs her family owned. That wasn't unusual, Kelsey thought as she checked her watch.

It was four twenty-five, time to put the casserole in.

The casserole was sitting on the top shelf in the refrigerator. Kelsey reached for it, turning over her mother's note as she did. There was a P.S. scribbled on the back. "Shawn Horton called. He'll call you back later."

Shawn Horton? Kelsey raised her eyebrows. He was a new senior at Spring Hill High, a pretty cute one. But even though girls were interested in him, he hadn't paid much attention to any of them. What could he want with her?

Still puzzled by the phone message, Kelsey put the casserole in the oven and set the timer. After imagining the wildest reasons for why he might have called, she calmed herself. "Wait a minute!" Kelsey laughed out loud. "Shawn Horton wouldn't have called me for a date!" Even if he had only been at school for three weeks, he would know not to waste his time on her. All the boys at Spring Hill High knew better than to ask Kelsey Kramer out.

It wasn't as if she were ugly or anything. With her shoulder-length sandy curls and hazel eyes, she fit right in with her popular group. They all agreed on clothes, makeup, and music, but there was one way in which Kelsey was different, and for that difference her friends thought she was crazy.

Sure, she had dated. But each date was worse

2

than the one before. Rick the Rat and Jon the Joker had proven the dating game wasn't worth the effort. They hadn't cared about her feelings at all. They had only been interested in using her for their own selfish purposes—such as making other girls jealous. Her friends had been shocked when Kelsey announced she was giving up boys, but since that declaration the month before her life had been peaceful.

So, it was curious that Shawn Horton would call, since he couldn't be calling for a date. He had to have another reason. . . . Maybe it was about what had happened in the school parking lot the day before.

Kelsey rolled her eyes, remembering. She had driven her mom's car to school and made one small mistake. She was a pretty good driver, but her parking skills weren't the best. She pulled in a little too close to the car next to her. And when she got out of the car, her door had bumped the car on her left. She had checked for paint scrapes and hadn't found any, but maybe she had overlooked them. Maybe she had even left a dent! What if Shawn were calling to accuse her? If her mom found out, she'd never let her use the car again for the rest of her life.

Kelsey jumped when the phone rang. How was she going to convince Shawn it had been an accident? It could be very embarrassing.

"Hello?" Her voice cracked.

3

"Kelsey? Are you OK?"

"Oh, Patty! I'm fine." She sighed with relief. She had almost forgotten Patty's promise to call. "Did it work? Did he ask you?"

"Yes!" Patty paused for dramatic effect. "I'm going to homecoming with the captain of the football team!"

Kelsey smiled to herself. She didn't have to ask for details. Patty was sure to tell her everything.

"I went by his locker after school, and just as I planned, I dropped that really heavy history book—"

"That's *so* corny!" Kelsey interrupted.

"Don't knock it! It worked. When we both leaned down to pick it up, we bumped heads and then our eyes met. It was too romantic. Cliff stared at me for a minute, and then he asked me to go with him to homecoming."

Kelsey wouldn't believe a story like that from anyone else. That sort of thing only happened on soap operas and to Patty. Patty, with her long dark hair and sparkling smile, was the most gorgeous girl in the junior class, and still she didn't trust her social life to fate. She schemed and plotted to get the right boyfriends and then schemed more in order to keep them. If the guys at Spring Hill High had any common sense, Kelsey reflected, someone like Patty wouldn't need to play games.

"Kelsey? Are you there?"

"Sure. Where would I have gone? I think it's great that you've got your date all lined up. I'm impressed!"

"Will you help me pick out a dress?" Patty asked.

"Of course." Kelsey loved shopping.

"Let's go whenever you're ready to get *your* dress," Patty suggested, a trace of a question in her voice.

"I'm not going to homecoming."

There was a silence at the other end of the line for a full minute. "Not going? I could get my brother to take you."

"No thanks." Kelsey had to laugh at the idea. "Your brother is a freshman in *college.* He'd probably rather die than take me to some high school dance."

"Really, I could get him to do it," Patty insisted. "When my parents were gone last weekend, he came home from school and had a party. I helped him clean up, so they wouldn't find out. He definitely owes me one."

"Thanks, but you don't need to waste your blackmail material on me. Missing the dance won't be the end of the world. I'll survive."

"If you're sure . . ." Patty didn't sound convinced.

"We've been through this before," Kelsey said firmly. "You know I'm sure. I don't waste my time on dates anymore!" She changed the subject casually. "How much do you know about Shawn Horton?"

"Besides the fact that he's drop-dead gorgeous?"

"Yeah, what is he besides kinda cute?" Kelsey asked.

"*Kinda cute?* That's like saying you're sort of blond. I heard he used to live in Hartsville," Patty said, naming a suburb several miles from Spring Hill. "He was their star quarterback, until he wrecked his knees last year. His family moved here over the summer. Since he had to give up sports, he's been modeling. Haven't you seen him in newspaper ads?"

"No, I don't think so," Kelsey answered. She was pleased to have more information about him. No one needed the FBI or the CIA when Patty was around. An interesting guy couldn't walk the halls of Spring Hill for more than a day before her friend knew all his vital statistics.

"Why do you ask, anyway?" Patty inquired. "Oh, never mind explaining. I think I know. While you've been telling the rest of us romance is stupid, you've been waiting for the best catch in the school."

"I thought Cliff Swensen was the best catch in the school," Kelsey teased. "Besides, I never said romance was stupid. I said it's overrated."

"And then you said you'd given up guys. So why the interest in Shawn?" Patty's voice was slightly hopeful.

"My mom left a message that he had called me. But she didn't say what he wanted."

"He's probably going to beg you to take up

men again and run off with him," Patty said, joking.

"*That* would only happen to you."

The girls didn't talk much longer. Patty was eager to phone all their other friends and relay the news about Kelsey's call from Shawn.

As Kelsey set the kitchen table, she let her mind wander. So, Shawn Horton was an ex-football player and a model. That was kind of an interesting combination. No wonder she'd seen girls drooling over him at school, smiling for all they were worth when they passed him in the halls. Maybe they wanted to get his attention, but she could do without it, especially if he were planning to chew her out for wrecking his car.

Kelsey sighed as she laid out the forks and then some salad bowls. If she had planned to scrape anyone's car, she wouldn't have picked a football player's, that much was for sure. They were OK at school, when she and her friends joked around with them, but Kelsey could tell that most of them thought they were too important for such human pursuits as friendship. They were on the bottom of the list of people she would turn to when she needed support and understanding.

And then, he had to be a model, too. He was probably as fussy about his car as he was about himself. A small dent would be as terrible as a scar to someone so wrapped up in appearances.

Kelsey pulled back a chair and sank into it. *I'm in deep trouble this time*, she thought grimly. *Shawn Horton won't let me off easily, but there is a bright side. If I don't survive the evening, I won't be able to take my chemistry quiz tomorrow!*

Just then the phone rang again, and Kelsey's mouth went dry. She had been lucky the first time. This second call had to be Shawn. With a shaky hand, she brought the receiver to her ear.

"Hello." She kept her voice low and deliberately calm.

"Could I speak to Kelsey, please?" The voice was polite.

"I'm Kelsey."

"This is Shawn Horton—from school." He paused before continuing. "I was wondering if I could stop by your house tonight about seven-thirty?"

Stop by? Did he want a paint sample from her mom's car, or what? She closed her eyes and summoned her courage. "Why?"

"I'm in Carson's history class, and we have to do a paper on local history. It's due a week from Monday, and I don't know anything about Spring Hill. He told me to talk to you."

"You want to know about my great-grandfather," she said quickly, smiling when she realized his call had nothing to do with her *or* her mother's car.

8

"I guess so." He sounded a little confused.

"Yeah. You want to talk to my mom about her grandfather, Gunnar Bjornson. He founded Spring Hill."

"Right. Look, I'm on a break, and I have to get back to work. Can you give me some fast directions to your house?"

Kelsey told Shawn the address, and he gave her a phone number, making her promise to call if it wasn't convenient for her parents to see him. She hung up the phone, shaking her head. Now that she was no longer in a panic, she could almost look forward to meeting this guy.

Kelsey's little brother was playing at a neighbor's house, her dad was reading the paper, and her mom was on the phone when the doorbell rang. She waited for one of her parents to make a move. Since Shawn wasn't a date, she didn't know how she was supposed to act. Besides that, she was out of practice with boys. Neither of her parents budged, and the bell chimed again. She had been hoping to stay out of the way of Shawn's visit with her mother, but now she found herself walking slowly to greet him.

The inside door was open, letting the cool evening breeze drift into the house. Shawn was leaning against the screen, his head bent down, so he could peer inside. His worn brown leather jacket was hanging open, showing a green shirt. A red notebook was tucked under his right arm. It looked as though he was ready to get to work.

"You're Kelsey," he said with a friendly smile as she approached.

"Yes—" She didn't know what else to say.

"I've seen you around school."

It gave her a little flutter to think he had noticed her when so many girls were flirting with him all the time. She told herself to stop being silly and open the door. He probably made it his business to notice every girl on principle.

When he stepped inside, Kelsey realized he was taller than she had expected. Her eyes were level with his chin. She could either look up into his face or glance down at his broad football shoulders.

Since he was there to see her mother, Kelsey didn't think Patty's dating rules applied. Without fluttering her lashes once, she tipped her head back and took a good look at the guy who was breaking hearts all over Spring Hill High.

Although she had seen him only from a distance at school, she could tell something was different about him that night. She squinted, trying to identify the change. He raised his eyebrows as if asking about her interest in his face. "You don't look like you do at school," she explained.

"I was doing a shoot, and they fixed my hair," he said. "I didn't want to be late for this appointment, so I didn't bother to wash it."

That certainly didn't fit the "model" image Kelsey had in her mind. She figured Shawn would always take time to look perfect, but here he was with plastered-down hair. His dark hair was fairly short on the sides and in the back, but the top was longer and it usually fell freely. That night it looked stiff and glued into place.

It was his eyes that fascinated her, though. They were greenish-brown, and seemed to reflect what he was thinking. Right then they said his full attention was focused on her, Kelsey Kramer. That was another surprise. She had expected him to charge into her house, get enough information for his paper, and then escape as quickly as possible. Instead he looked as if he were happy to be there. Maybe she was imagining it.

Kelsey's mom came into the hall and looked from Shawn to Kelsey. "Is this Shawn?" she asked. "Sorry to keep you waiting, but Jill had questions about the guest list. The wedding is exciting, but I'll be glad when it's over."

Shawn wrinkled his forehead. Kelsey explained. "My older brother's getting married—to Jill." More under her breath she added, "And we'll all be glad when it's over."

He smiled at her before he turned to her mother. "I'm Shawn Horton, Mrs. Kramer. I appreciate your taking time to talk with me." He shifted the notebook and shook hands first with Mrs. Kramer and then Mr. Kramer, who had also joined them.

"So you want to hear about the Bjornsons," Mr. Kramer said, leading them into the living room.

Kelsey was surprised. The Kramer living room was usually reserved for business acquaintances and relatives. Her parents must be taking Shawn and his project seriously, but then her mother always did love talking about family history.

Shawn sat on a sectional sofa that curved around the far corner of the room. He didn't look so tall when he sank into the cushions. Kelsey's mom also sat on the sofa, and her dad chose an adjacent chair. That left only one chair for Kelsey, unless she slipped into the spot on the sofa between Shawn and her mother.

Kelsey settled into the straight-backed chair and tried to get comfortable. Shawn looked relaxed. The spiral notebook was balanced across his knees, and he was chewing on his pen while he waited for Mrs. Kramer to begin talking.

"My grandfather, Gunnar Bjornson, came to America in eighteen ninety-nine, when he was twenty years old," she began. "Some of his cousins had already settled in Minnesota, and their letters back to Sweden made America sound like a land of infinite opportunities. Gunnar was an adventurer, and he decided to seek his fortune across the ocean. . . ."

Kelsey tuned her mother out. She had heard the story many times before. Shawn, however, was scribbling notes about Gunnar's hopes for his new life. His eyes were fastened on Mrs. Kramer as he listened attentively.

"He was working on a cousin's farm when he met Inga. She was just nineteen when they got married. . . ."

Nineteen. That would be three years from now for me! Kelsey thought with amazement. *I can't even imagine it. At the rate I'm going, considering the way I feel about guys and romance and everything, I probably won't get married at all.*

"They homesteaded a plot of land some distance from his relatives' farm. He built her a small house on a hill next to a lake—"

"Was that in Spring Hill?" Shawn asked.

"Yes—"

"Let me guess," he interrupted. "A hill by a lake. Was their house on the hill where the high school is now?"

"That very spot," Mrs. Kramer said with a smile. Kelsey could tell her mother liked Shawn. She always liked people who shared an interest in the past. She could talk for hours on the subject.

"Other farmers began to settle in the surrounding area, and a young man from St. Paul built a general store. Since Gunnar had been the first settler, and he was a take-charge kind of man, he encouraged everyone to work together. My father was their second son, and by the time he was ten years old, a small village had grown up in the center of the farms."

Kelsey found Shawn much more interesting than the next chapter of her mother's story. She noticed the square shape of Shawn's jaw. When he really got going taking notes, she could see the muscles tighten, and she bet he was clenching his teeth. He looked like a determined person. Patty would say he had an athlete's face, except that his nose was too straight. Most of the football players at Spring Hill High had broken their noses by the time they were sophomores.

"Would you like something to eat? We have some dessert left from dinner," her mother offered. Kelsey realized she had managed to miss the conclusion of her mother's history review.

"I'd love some," he answered enthusiastically.

Kelsey was surprised—again. He could easily have made an excuse and left. He had to have other things to do. Modeling must take up a lot of his time. But instead, he walked beside her to the kitchen. It was flattering, and Kelsey felt suddenly shy. For the life of her, she couldn't think of anything to say to him, so she hurried to help her mother slice four pieces of cake, then she served it to her dad and Shawn.

Just then the back door burst open, and Kelsey's younger brother sprinted into the kitchen. "Cake?"

Kelsey walked back to the counter to cut another piece. Her brother grabbed it and plopped into a chair at the table where Shawn was attacking his dessert as though he hadn't eaten in weeks. Kelsey slipped into the seat next to him.

"Hi, I'm Tommy. Who are you?"

Shawn looked up, with crumbs still caught on his lips. "I'm Shawn Horton."

"Are you Kelsey's new boyfriend?" Before Shawn could say anything, Tommy answered his own question. "You can't be. She doesn't have boyfriends anymore."

Kelsey kicked Tommy under the table as Shawn looked at her, a question in his expressive eyes. She tried to change the subject. "More cake?" she offered brightly.

"That would be great. I didn't have time for dinner."

Before Kelsey could push her chair back from the table, her mother jumped to her feet and brought him the last piece. "Would you like some milk, too?"

"Yes, please."

Kelsey's mother loved to care for stray cats and dogs—not that Shawn Horton fit into that category, Kelsey thought. He must have a mother who could feed him. It was hard to believe he had been so anxious to work on his history report that he skipped dinner to rush to their house. Now *that* was conscientious!

He finished the cake, chugged the glass of milk, and pulled a napkin from the holder on the table to wipe the white mustache from his lips. His hands were large, with slim, strong

15

fingers. Kelsey could imagine them wrapped around a football. He *looked* like an athlete, but he didn't act like one, at least not like the athletes *she* knew.

Suddenly Kelsey realized she was gazing right into Shawn's green sparkling eyes, and he'd caught her staring. It wasn't her style to check out guys, especially since she'd given them up. She would have been embarrassed at getting caught in the act, but Shawn's open grin and his relaxed manner kept her from feeling shy. He smiled, and she smiled back. *Funny,* she thought, *I would never have predicted that I'd be sitting around tonight eating cake with Shawn Horton. I thought I'd be studying for my chemistry quiz. . . .*

"My homework," she groaned, shoving the last cake crumbs around her plate with a fork.

"Have I been keeping you from something?" Shawn asked, carrying his dish and glass to the sink.

"Just a quiz in chemistry, my worst class."

"I could help you."

Kelsey dropped her fork. It didn't just fall out of her hand onto her plate; it clattered to the floor and bounced. The picture of Shawn tutoring her was just too much. He had to have more exciting and glamorous prospects for the evening. He sounded as if he'd sincerely like to stick around with her, but Kelsey decided he was only being polite. Nothing made sense. "Thanks, but I can handle it myself."

"OK, but I was pretty good at chemistry last year. And I feel guilty that I took up so much of your time tonight."

"It was nothing," Mrs. Kramer answered on Kelsey's behalf. "If you need any more information, just give us a call. I could dig out some old photographs, if they would help."

"Thank you," he said appreciatively. "I may need to see those pictures to finish my report."

"Well, you're welcome anytime, Shawn."

Kelsey accompanied Shawn as he walked back into the living room and pulled his jacket off the back of the sofa. After he slipped his arms into it, he pulled the collar up. A minute before, sitting at the table, he might have been a member of Kelsey's family. But then standing in his jacket he looked like a model or a Super Bowl quarterback—Kelsey wasn't sure which.

Shawn turned to her. They were standing very close.

"I appreciated your hanging around tonight, Kelsey. Talking to someone else's parents can be kind of rough."

Kelsey nodded. Somehow she found that confession really appealing. Shawn Horton didn't look like someone who would be intimidated by her mother. He was so nice—and so cute.

"No problem," she murmured. "I've got to go study my chemistry now."

"OK. I'll see you around school."

It would sure raise Patty's eyebrows if Shawn Horton really did wave to her in the hall or something! Kelsey smiled at the idea as she ran up the stairs two at a time while her mother told Shawn good-bye. She heard a snatch of their conversation.

"Was I able to help you?" Mrs. Kramer asked.

"Definitely," he answered. "I think I'll write about the changes that took place when the plant was built after World War II in Spring Hill."

"Good choice. In fact, I've got . . ."

Kelsey would have stood outside her door and listened longer, but she knew her chemistry was waiting. She couldn't ignore it all night. Somehow, though, she had a feeling that she wasn't going to be able to concentrate very well. With Shawn Horton on her mind—chemistry couldn't really compete.

Chapter Two

"Shawn Horton was at your house last night?"

Patty's words were too loud. They echoed in the early-morning hall, and kids on their way to class turned to stare.

Kelsey felt her cheeks heating up. Her summer tan had faded, and she knew the blush must be showing up fire-engine red on her fair skin.

She looked from Patty to their other two friends—petite red-haired Barb and Cheryl, looking preppy as usual. They were all waiting with wide eyes for Kelsey to tell the story.

"Look, he came over to talk to my mom. He needed a topic for his history paper in Carson's class."

"And then what happened?" Cheryl asked. "The suspense is killing me!"

"He took notes, ate some cake, and went home," Kelsey said dryly.

"You mean Shawn Horton was sitting at the same table where we eat pizza in your house?" Barb rolled her eyes as if it were just too much to imagine.

"Yeah." Kelsey was beginning to feel mischievous. "He sat in the chair you always use."

"I'm going to faint," Barb declared. "Do I look like I'm going to faint?"

"No, you don't," Patty said, taking charge of the interrogation. "Now tell us more about him."

"There's not much to tell! He was nice." It sounded pretty stupid, saying Shawn Horton was nice, but Kelsey couldn't think of a better way to describe him. He'd been friendly to her, polite to her parents, and he hadn't even seemed to hate Tommy on sight as most of her friends did.

"Nice? How nice? Give us an example!" Patty demanded.

"Well, he offered to help me study for my chemistry quiz," Kelsey confided.

"Studying with him must have been an unforgettable experience," Cheryl said, a tinge of awe in her voice.

"Actually, I didn't take him up on it. I was sure he had better things to do," Kelsey explained.

"Only Kelsey-who-hates-boys would turn down a chance like that," Patty said in disgust. "I would have taken time to find out if there was any chemistry between me and Shawn Horton!"

Barb giggled.

"Anyone would. Even Kelsey," Cheryl declared. "I don't think she's telling the truth. I bet Shawn Horton never set foot in her house."

"He was there. . . ." Kelsey told them, rising to their bait.

"Prove it," Cheryl challenged.

Her friends' heads suddenly snapped to the left. Kelsey followed their stares and found herself face to face with Shawn. The girls had completely forgotten that his locker was just a few down from Barb's, where they were standing. *And here we are shouting his name at the top of our lungs!* Kelsey thought, mortified. Her cheeks turned pink again.

"Hi, Kelsey." Shawn flashed her a broad, friendly grin. Kelsey gazed into his eyes, mesmerized. He looked really happy to see her; she felt as though his smile was for her and her alone.

"Good morning, Shawn."

"Thanks again for last night." He started to move away. "See you later, and good luck on the chemistry test," he called over his shoulder.

"Believe me now?" Kelsey asked her friends triumphantly. Saying they were in shock would have been an understatement. Patty's mouth was hanging open, and Barb was rubbing her eyes as if she expected to wake up from a dream.

"Yeah, we believe you," Cheryl said breathlessly. She checked her watch. It was time to head to their first class. "Are you going to the game tonight?"

There was a football game that evening, but Kelsey wasn't in the mood to watch her friends hit on guys for dates to homecoming. "I can't go. My brother and Jill are coming over for dinner. We're having wedding discussions or something."

"Your favorite topic—the wedding." Patty was sympathetic. She understood how Kelsey felt about being surrounded by all that love and romance.

"Really. It can't be over soon enough for me," Kelsey agreed wholeheartedly.

Kelsey moved around the dining room table, feeling comfortable in her worn blue sweat suit. She stepped back for a minute and adjusted her glasses on her nose. After having studied late the night before, her contacts had been bothering her.

"Mom, I think you had me set too many places," Kelsey called into the kitchen.

"I don't think so," her mother answered. "There are the four of us. Plus Eric and Jill make six, and Shawn makes seven."

"Shawn?" she whispered. "Shawn Horton is coming to dinner?"

"I invited him last night. Didn't I mention it?"

"I guess you forgot." *Oh, no,* Kelsey groaned inwardly. *Shawn is coming to dinner, and I look like I crawled out from under a rock.*

Quickly she zipped up her sweatshirt to cover the faded T-shirt underneath. She brushed imaginary dust off her pants. She considered dashing upstairs to change, but that seemed too much like something her friends would do. Kelsey Kramer wasn't supposed to care. Besides, Shawn wasn't coming to see her; he was just working on his history paper.

The doorbell rang. Kelsey knew it had to be Shawn. Jill and her brother would use the back door.

"Don't make him stand outside," her mother said. "It's turned chilly out there."

If she let him freeze on her doorstep, it would be all over school on Monday, Kelsey thought. The guys at Spring Hill High who enjoyed talking about their "cold" dates with Kelsey Kramer would probably love to hear that Shawn had gotten the same treatment.

The doorbell buzzed impatiently, and Kelsey's mom stuck her head out of the kitchen. "What *are* you doing?"

"Answering the door," she said with a sigh of resignation.

When she opened the door, Shawn was huddled with his back to the wind, his arms crossed over his chest, and his hands tucked out of sight.

"Come in and warm up," Kelsey said, feeling a little bit bad for making him wait.

"Thanks." Shawn crossed the threshold quickly, running his fingers through his hair. "It's really starting to get cold out there," he observed cheerfully.

Kelsey nonchalantly stood back to sneak a good look at him, from his windblown hair down to his white socks and loafers. This was the Shawn Horton she knew from school.

Kelsey smiled feebly. Backing away, she said, "Why don't you make yourself at home in the living room? I've got to help my mother in the kitchen."

"Maybe I can help, too," he said, tagging behind her.

She stopped dead in her tracks. "You're kidding! You really want to?"

"Sure." His eyes told her he was serious.

Kelsey shook her head and led the way to the kitchen. Shawn Horton wasn't an average guy, she reminded herself.

Her mother put them both to work. While Kelsey popped dinner rolls into the microwave, Shawn put fried chicken on a platter. He held the strainer, while she drained the water off the vegetables.

"What a team," he said as she dumped the peas and carrots into a bowl.

"My sister doesn't like boys," whined a familiar voice.

24

"Tommy," Kelsey said through gritted teeth, "why don't you go take your camera apart or something?"

"Because I'm hungry."

A draft of cool air hit Kelsey, and suddenly the kitchen was bustling with new bodies and voices. Eric and Jill had come in the back door. Between welcoming hugs, Kelsey managed to introduce Shawn to her brother and his pretty, blue-eyed, fluffy-haired fiancée. Eric and Jill had been together for a couple of years now, but Kelsey didn't know her all that well. What she did know was that Jill couldn't have been sweeter or more pleasant. And she and Eric adored each other so much it was nauseating, at least in Kelsey's opinion.

With Jill lending a hand in her usual fashion—Eric had vacated the kitchen as quickly as possible in *his* usual fashion—they got the rest of the dinner on the table in a matter of minutes. There was only one tense moment, when Shawn and Kelsey both went for the rolls in the microwave at the same time. Their hands brushed, and Kelsey blushed; but then Shawn laughed, and Kelsey had to laugh, too.

Soon they were all settled at the table. Kelsey ended up sitting with Jill on one side and Shawn on the other. Eric was across the table, so he could stare at Jill. Tommy was next to Eric, and her parents were at either end of the table. It was a little crowded, and much too cozy, in

Kelsey's opinion, who was very aware of Shawn's leg touching hers.

"Why aren't you at the Spring Hill football game tonight?" Eric asked his sister as he passed the vegetables to Mr. Kramer.

"I didn't want to go." Kelsey bit into a roll, hoping that by keeping her mouth full she could discourage the conversation.

No such luck. "You and your friends always went to the games—out of loyalty to Spring Hill High." Eric repeated what Kelsey had told him the last fall.

"Well, I didn't want to go tonight," she said stubbornly.

Leave it to her big brother to raise embarrassing issues. That was nothing new. She didn't plan on explaining in front of Shawn that she was staying home because her friends would spend the whole evening flirting and plotting their homecoming strategies.

"Not everyone goes to the games," she continued, trying to defend herself without saying too much. "Shawn used to *play* football, but he's not rushing off to the game."

"Shawn has a reason," her brother said, giving her a glance that made her feel as if she'd said something incredibly ignorant.

At first Kelsey couldn't think what Shawn's reason could be, and her brother didn't elaborate.

"You knew I played football?" Shawn asked Eric.

"Yeah. My college roommate is the assistant coach at Hartsville. He worked with your older brother, and he was so excited to have you quarterbacking the Hartsville team that I went to a few games. It was really a shame you had to quit playing. You were something else."

"Thanks. I liked all the coaches at Hartsville." Shawn's voice was low.

Kelsey looked up at him, but he was staring at his plate. He wouldn't let her read his eyes this time. Now she knew what Eric had been referring to—the injury that had ended Shawn's football career. Probably the last thing he wanted to do at this point was watch other people play. With a shrug, Kelsey turned her attention back to her dinner.

"Kelsey, don't forget we have the dress fittings tomorrow morning," Jill said brightly.

"How could I forget?" She tried to match Jill's cheerful tone, but she was too busy attempting to pick the chicken off the bone with a knife and fork. It was fine for Tommy to pick up a chicken leg in his hands, but she could hardly do the same, considering the company. If her mother had to invite Shawn to dinner, she could at least have served something easier to eat!

"You don't have to sound so excited about the dresses," Eric teased. "We know how you feel about romance and mushy stuff, but it means a lot to both of us to have you in the wedding."

"Hey, no problem," she said quickly, abandoning her chicken in favor of concentrating on a mound of potato salad. She was starting to get very tired of the comments being made about her decision not to date, even if her family was only kidding. No one understood how she felt. They hadn't been there when Rick Smithline dumped her at a party because his old girlfriend decided she wanted him back. They hadn't been stuck laughing at Jon Rossiter's bad jokes on three dates—bad jokes of which she was usually the target. Frankly, she could find better things to do with her time.

The rest of the dinner conversation focused on the wedding plans. Kelsey was relieved that Jill was now the center of attention. Shawn ate his food and smiled at Kelsey from time to time. She was amazed that all the wedding talk didn't make him squirm. It certainly made her want to wiggle in her chair.

"Let's move into the family room," Kelsey's mother suggested as the last of the dessert disappeared from their plates. "I've put the photos in there for Shawn."

"Sounds fun, Mom, but we've got to meet with the musicians we hired for the reception," Eric explained, his arm wrapped around Jill's waist. They were nearly out the back door, when Jill turned back.

"Remember, Kelsey. I'm picking you up at eleven o'clock tomorrow."

"OK," she said, managing a weak smile.

Kelsey, Mrs. Kramer, and Shawn moved to the comfortable plaid couch in the family room. Mr. Kramer had excused himself to work in his den, but Kelsey knew he was really watching TV. Tommy had slipped away to his room, to her great relief.

A battered shoe box was sitting on the coffee table. Mrs. Kramer had sorted the old photographs, making a pile of pictures from the time period that Shawn had chosen for his report. He seemed fascinated with the dim black-and-white snapshots of the plant being built. One picture caught Kelsey's attention.

It showed the completed factory with a family standing in front of it. Kelsey held it out toward her mother, pointing at a small girl in a sailor dress. "Is this you?"

"Yes." Her mom laughed. "I don't remember the opening ceremonies, but my mother always said my older brothers ran around like monkeys and drove all the guests crazy."

Kelsey took the picture back and stared at it. It was hard to believe those two young boys with missing teeth had grown up to be her uncles—the ones who ruffled her hair and called her "Little Kelsey" every time they visited. Had they really been obnoxious kids, like Tommy?

"You're enjoying this, too, aren't you?" Shawn whispered.

"I guess I am," she admitted.

The grandfather clock chimed, and her mother

jumped. "It's getting late. I have to run to the store for a few things before it closes. Will you two be all right here?"

"Sure," Shawn answered before Kelsey could say a thing. "I'm almost finished with the photographs. They're really giving me an idea of the time period. Thanks a lot."

"You're welcome," Mrs. Kramer answered as she gathered up her purse and coat. "It was nice to share them with someone."

A minute later they heard the car start. Kelsey's mother pulled out of the driveway. Shawn stacked the photographs and set them back in the box. "Your mom is pretty special."

"She really is," Kelsey agreed. They sat on the couch, side by side, and neither one talked. For a moment it reminded Kelsey of some of her dates, when she and the guy had run out of things to say. That was possibly the worst sensation in the world. But Shawn wasn't a date. He had come to see her mother, and he'd be leaving, now that his research was finished. He could hardly want to hang around any longer with a girl dressed in sweat clothes and glasses. "I suppose you have someplace to go tonight?"

"I don't have any plans, actually, unless you want to jigsaw."

"What?" Kelsey couldn't help sounding surprised, and her tone took Shawn aback for a moment.

"I saw a jigsaw puzzle on that table in the corner," he explained with a sheepish shrug. "Do you like puzzles as much as I do?"

Kelsey grinned. "I'm addicted to them, but that one's a real killer," she warned. "It's a bowl of popcorn that's been tipped over. All the pieces are kernels of popcorn and things. We've been working on it since last weekend."

"I'm willing to help." She looked skeptical, and he added, "If you don't mind. I'm sure *you* have someplace to go. I should be leaving." He started to stand up.

"If I don't mind?" Kelsey repeated with a laugh. She put a hand on Shawn's arm to stop him. This time her grin was mischievous. "I bet I can find more pieces in five minutes than you can. . . ." She felt giddy. He wanted to hang around!

"You're on!" Accepting the challenge, Shawn pushed up his sleeves and walked over to the table.

She snapped on the overhead light in the corner, and they got to work. The bowl was already put together; Kelsey and her mom had done that over the weekend. Shawn found a place for the first piece he tried.

"Beginner's luck," she teased.

"How do you know I'm not a champion puzzler?"

They both had been leaning over the table, and now they were nearly face to face. She smiled shyly. "I guess I don't know." They held each other's eyes for a long moment.

"I like your glasses," he said, changing the subject. "They match your eyes."

That was what Kelsey had thought when she chose them, but nobody had ever noticed before. "I don't wear them very often, but I guess I like them, too." She shrugged and pushed back a stray wisp of sandy blond hair.

"Could I ask you something?"

Scanning the loose puzzle pieces for a half-popped kernel, she told him, "Go ahead."

"I was wondering if you could tell me what your brothers meant by some of the things they were saying about you."

Kelsey swallowed. She let the wisp of hair fall back over her glasses, so she could hide behind it. Did she want to discuss her dating theory with Shawn Horton? No chance. Maybe if she ignored his question, he'd forget about it.

But Shawn didn't give up that easily. "They made it sound like you hate guys. Do you?"

Kelsey looked up and was startled by the concern in Shawn's eyes. "No, of course I don't hate guys."

"Then, what were they trying to tell me?"

She turned a puzzle piece around a few times, examining it more closely than she needed to. She wasn't sure how much she wanted to share with Shawn. "I guess you could say I've given up dating," she managed finally.

Shawn looked mystified. "But why?"

"I just got tired of all the games," she said with a sigh. It was easier than she'd expected to be honest with him. Patty had shrieked when she told her about the new Kelsey Kramer, as if that made Kelsey some kind of freak. Shawn was showing much more sense and sympathy by simply asking her why.

She met his thoughtful green eyes, suddenly wanting to tell him more. "You know, getting dates and falling in love is all my friends talk about. I've tried it, but I just don't think it's worth the effort it takes. So, I decided to give it up."

"Forever?" he asked.

"Probably not *forever*," she admitted with a wry smile. She hadn't told her friends that yet. Patty would be relieved that Kelsey hadn't developed some kind of permanent condition.

"I know what you mean about the games." Shawn nodded. "You're right, they're stupid. But don't you have some friends who just happen to be guys?"

"I guess I do," she said casually. She usually got to know the boys her friends were dating, but she wasn't sure she'd call them friends.

"I need help!" The cry came from upstairs. Shawn jumped to his feet, but before he could take a step, Tommy thundered down the stairs into the family room, wires and things in his hands. "I took my remote-control car apart, and now I have too many pieces left over."

Kelsey grimaced. Why did ten-year-old brothers have to be such a constant pain?

"Can I see it?" Shawn asked.

"Sure." Tommy dropped the car on the table, on top of the puzzle, and handed the loose wires and screws to Shawn. Kelsey knew why her little brother was smiling. He had found someone who would pay attention to him. She caught his eye and tried to communicate to him by a glare that she'd appreciate it if he vacated the family room immediately. Tommy stuck out his tongue.

Shawn pried the bottom off the car and poked around inside it. It wasn't long before the extra pieces were gone, and he handed the now-working car back to Tommy.

"Gee, thanks." Tommy was clearly impressed. "Hey, guys. Can I help with the puzzle?"

They said "No!" in unison.

Tommy knew when he had been beaten. "That's OK, it's time for *Adventure Jack*." Kelsey's brother waited all week for the continuing story that aired on a local radio station. She could hardly believe he would have missed it to work on a puzzle with her and Shawn. It looked as though Tommy had a new buddy.

After Tommy left, Kelsey wasn't sure she should have insisted so vehemently on his departure. Which would have been better, Tommy's nonstop chatter or Shawn's further questions about her social life? She bent her head to study the puzzle.

Shawn laughed. "You don't have to ignore me. I'll stop being so nosey."

She sat back in her chair, surprised. Football types were supposed to have more determination and less sensitivity. She had expected him to grill her like a lawyer. "You will?"

"Yeah." Shawn fitted a piece into the puzzle and winked at Kelsey. His tone was serious, though. "I don't want to make you uncomfortable."

Uncomfortable? *Anything but,* Kelsey thought to herself. It was true that it had been a little embarrassing to have to explain her dating dilemma to Shawn, but for the most part she felt really comfortable with him. He was easy to talk to, not like most of the boys she had spent time with. She'd already told him things she hadn't even shared with her girlfriends.

"That's nice of you," she said lightly.

"Hey, no problem. It's really not hard to be nice to a nice girl!"

"Thanks." Kelsey laughed, and Shawn grinned, then made a production of stretching out his right arm to check his wristwatch. "Time's up. I win!"

"You rat!" she cried. She had been tricked by his charm. "You asked me all that stuff about dating just to distract me."

"No, I didn't," he said honestly. "I asked be-

cause I wanted to know how you felt about—
things." He cocked his head to one side and
narrowed his deep greenish-brown eyes. "Since
you're not seeing anybody special these days,
maybe we could . . ."

Maybe we could what? Kelsey's palms were
sweating. She realized she was terrified Shawn
might ask her out.

"Maybe we could say 'hi' to each other at
school." Shawn smiled. "If it doesn't go against
your principles, that is."

Kelsey felt relieved and foolish. Of course someone like Shawn Horton wouldn't ask her for a
date. She wiped her hands on her sweat pants
and smiled back at him. "I'd be pretty insulted
if you passed me in the hall and didn't say
anything!"

"What if I sat with you at lunch one day?"

Kelsey wrinkled her upturned nose and pretended to consider. "My friends might move
over and make room for you." *If they didn't
faint first,* she added to herself.

"Does this make us friends?" Shawn was still
joking with her, but Kelsey could read serious-
ness in his eyes. Were they friends? she wondered. People didn't consciously decide to be
friends. Friends just happened. And something
had happened with Shawn. She liked being with
him, they had fun together. "I guess we are!"

He stood up and stretched. Looking at him,
Kelsey was reminded of the fact that this guy

was a model. Patty had been right. He *was* drop-dead gorgeous. Meanwhile, she wasn't exactly glamorous, that night or any night. A girl Shawn could be friends with, sure, but she could probably consider herself safe as far as romance was concerned.

"Well, I have to get home. My mother says she never sees me anymore. Walk me to the door?"

As she closed the front door behind him, Kelsey's first impulse was to call Patty. She got as far as taking the phone off the hook before realizing her friends wouldn't be home from the football game. She didn't really mind. Patty and Barb and Cheryl might not understand how she felt about Shawn. For now, he was going to be her secret.

Chapter Three

"Don't you love your dress?" Sandy, Jill's college roommate, turned to Kelsey and another woman in the dressing room at the Spring Hill bridal salon.

"I think it's great," Sue, a friend of Jill's from the office, agreed enthusiastically. She was tall, with wheat-colored hair, while Sandy was dark haired and small.

Kelsey felt the other two bridesmaids looking at her, and she gave them a weak smile. Right then she couldn't breathe deeply or talk, unless she wanted the seamstress to stick a pin into her.

She looked at herself in the mirror. The dress *was* pretty, and it was a perfect color for her. The royal-blue satin made her eyes come alive. She raised a hand to her bare neck, where the choker of pearls would go.

"Please, honey, don't move," the seamstress reminded her.

"Sorry." Kelsey studied her reflection some more. The neckline was lower than on any dress she'd ever worn before. Jill had called it a sweetheart neck. Kelsey liked the way the bodice was cut down from each shoulder at an angle that came to a graceful point in the center, and she liked the full, puffy sleeves. She held her breath while the seamstress tightened the cuffs above the elbows to help the sleeves keep their balloon shape.

Actually, the dress looked a lot like the one Patty had worn to the prom the year before. Her dress had been soft pink, with sleeves and a neck cut the same, but it didn't have a big bow on the back. Jill said bridesmaids' dresses had to look interesting in back since that was all anyone would see of them during the ceremony. That might be true, but Kelsey didn't know how she'd be able to sit down at the reception without crushing her bow.

"I wonder how Jill's doing," said Sue.

"As soon as Kelsey's done with her fitting, we can all go over to her dressing room," Sandy said.

"You can go now," the seamstress told them, gathering her measuring tape and pins. "I'm finished, unless one of you plans to eat too much pizza between now and the wedding."

They all hurried to pull on their jeans and

sweaters, so they could see Jill before she took off her wedding dress. After knocking on the door to her room, they sneaked inside.

"Oh, you're beautiful," Sue whispered.

"The dress is gorgeous!" raved Sandy.

"They're right," was all Kelsey could think of to say. Jill looked like a princess in white lace and ruffles. The train was fanned out behind her while a woman marked changes in the hem.

"So, how are the plans progressing?" Sandy asked, perched on the bench in the corner. Sue sat down, too. Kelsey stayed back by herself, feeling suddenly shy. What did she know about weddings?

"I think everything's under control," Jill told them, holding up a hand to show her crossed fingers.

"Do you have something old and something new?" asked Sandy teasingly.

"And something borrowed and something blue?" Sue added.

"Are you having a bride and groom on top of the cake?"

"How are the invitations coming along?"

Kelsey's head was swimming.

"The invitations?" Jill laughed as another woman pulled the veil over her face. "We thought we were just about done with them, but the guest list seems to get longer every day. You know you can't forget anyone—not my father's first business partner or Eric's long-lost great-aunt."

"Really," Sue said seriously. "My cousin innocently forgot to invite her mother's old bridge partners, and now none of them are speaking to her mother."

"Have you chosen the flowers?" Sandy asked.

"Yes. I'll be carrying white roses, and you'll all have pink roses and something white—I forget what they're called. Then there are the flowers for the church and centerpieces for the reception."

"I was shopping last night, and I saw the china pattern you chose. It's beautiful. Maybe someday *I'll* be choosing china and wedding invitations!" Sandy said, with a dry laugh.

Kelsey looked at her. Somehow Sandy didn't sound as if she were joking, as if she thought there were anything funny about waiting for her turn to get married.

A shocking thought popped into Kelsey's mind. Didn't the games *ever* stop? Her friends spent hours dreaming about falling in love, and they took nearly as much time scheming to get dates. Kelsey had figured that was a temporary phase she could skip, but what if the games went on forever? Jill's roommate was still dreaming. And now that Jill had found someone to marry, she had to spend days picking out dresses and flowers for the wedding, china, and who-knows-what-else for their new home. It was scary.

"What about the band for the reception? Is it a good dance band?" Sue wanted to know.

"They're dynamite," Jill assured her. "Eric and I heard them at another wedding."

"Our dresses will be great for dancing. Can you picture the full skirts swishing when we move?" Sue grinned at the thought.

They could think about their skirts flouncing while they danced, Kelsey told herself. *I'll be sitting with my parents.*

"That reminds me, Kelsey"—Jill turned to look at her—"you should invite someone your own age. You'll need a date when the dancing starts, unless you have some cousins you wouldn't mind as partners."

"I think I'll skip the cousins and the date, if no one minds," she said, stuffing her hands in her jeans pockets. She felt insecure around these older, wiser women but tried her best to look cool and unconcerned.

"What's wrong with the gorgeous hunk you brought to dinner last night?" Jill asked, letting out her breath as the fitter undid the buttons at the back of her gown.

"Jill! I didn't invite him to dinner," Kelsey said firmly.

"Well, he wasn't looking at *me* with those sexy green eyes."

"*Ooooh,*" the others cried teasingly.

"Give me a break," Kelsey exclaimed. She was glad the lights in the dressing room were so bright that they washed out her blush.

"OK. But he is cute," Jill said, sounding as if she were going to drop the subject. Then she added, "Eric said it's too bad about his football career coming to an end so quickly. I guess he was really some quarterback."

"Well, he's got new things to do. He's a model now," Kelsey pointed out. She, for one, didn't think it was such a tragedy that Shawn couldn't play football any longer. He didn't strike Kelsey as a charity case.

"A model—" Sue winked at Sandy.

"He's just a friend. Honest, that's all he is," Kelsey told them sternly.

"If you say so, Kelsey!" said Jill.

Kelsey dipped her brush into a can of red paint and started to fill in the large *C* at the beginning of the banner for Friday's football game. Spring Hill would be playing the Centerville Hawks.

Cage the Hawks was outlined in bold letters on the long paper stretched across the cafeteria floor. Barb was painting the *G*, while Patty tried to sketch a sickly looking hawk at the far end. They expected Cheryl to join them any minute, after cheerleading practice.

"Kelsey, entertain us with stories about the big wedding," Patty called from her post at the other end of the banner.

Kelsey sat back on her heels and took a deep breath. The school cafeteria floor was *not* a comfortable place to kneel.

"We got our bridesmaids' dresses fitted on Saturday. They're really pretty, but you should see Jill's wedding dress. It's incredible."

"Too bad she's wasting it on your brother," Barb said, looking up from her work for just a second. "I mean, no offense, but Jill sounds really nice. Why would she want to marry anyone so mean and insensitive?"

"Really," Patty added. "I couldn't believe the way he teased you about Rick Smithline last summer. He was really a jerk."

"I agree," Kelsey said emphatically. "And you guys don't know the half of it!" Whenever she had been naive enough to confide in her brother, her secrets had always come back to haunt her in the form of jokes. "I keep telling myself, though, that he's just your standard obnoxious big brother. I mean, none of you has one, so we don't have anyone to compare him to! Still, I'm going to ask Jill about Eric someday. If she really loves *him*, then romance is something I don't need in my life!"

"Sometimes I don't blame you for your theories about guys," Patty said, her forehead furrowed, as she concentrated on her painting. "With brothers like yours, you haven't had the greatest role models."

"Are we discussing Kelsey's brothers?" Cheryl asked, dropping her books by the wall and then kneeling next to Barb.

"Yes, we are," Kelsey told her. "Patty and Barb have agreed they're two of the strangest guys on this earth."

"You're not kidding. Has Tommy broken anything lately? My cassette player has never been the same since the day he decided to figure out how it worked," Cheryl said.

"He hasn't changed a bit, although my dad says it's just a phase and he'll grow out of it. My mom actually *encourages* him. She thinks he's going to turn out to be some kind of genius. What a joke! Last night, he tried to repair the bathroom radio. He claimed it sounded fuzzy. Well, that was better than the way it sounds now—"

"Let me guess," Patty interrupted. "I bet it doesn't work at all."

"You're right. I put my makeup on in silence this morning."

They all groaned at the thought of doing their faces without the chatter of Lewis and Jackson's morning show. Then Patty directed the conversation to a new course. "Barb, tell us again what Mark said when he asked you to homecoming."

Kelsey dipped her brush back into the paint can, hoping to tune out Barb's cheerful tale by concentrating on the banner. She knew her friend would repeat the big invitation scene word for word, and she had already heard the story twice.

"I'd planned to do everything you told me, Patty, but he was waiting for me outside my math class. . . ." Barb stopped to giggle, and Kelsey realized painting wouldn't save her. She was going to hear it all again.

"He followed me to the drinking fountain, then he stood behind me so I couldn't get past him after I'd had a drink. I thought it was pretty strange until he said, really fast, 'Will you go to homecoming with me?' "

"Did you just melt?" Cheryl asked, pushing up her sleeves, so no paint would get on her sweater.

"I thought I was going to die," Barb assured them all. "Hey, Kelsey," she called. "You dated Mark. Do you think I should get a fluffy, feminine dress, or should I go for something glamorous? Which would he like better?"

"Either one. He sure didn't notice what I was wearing on our date!"

When Kelsey had dated, most guys had lasted three dates before they found a reason not to ask her out again. Mark had been different. Their one date had been a disaster from the minute they got to the movie theater. He took her to one of those everybody-gets-killed movies. Determined not to complain, she planned to ignore the film and eat the popcorn. When she reached into the tub they were supposed to be sharing, it was empty. He had eaten it all! Later, they suffered silently through hamburgers and fries. Once they finished talking about his car, there had been nothing left to say.

Kelsey decided that very night that she had wasted enough time flirting and primping and smiling at guys. They weren't worth the effort. Mark had been her last date.

"We'll meet after school on Wednesday to help Barb pick out a dress," Patty declared. "Kelsey, you should come with us. You might still get invited to the dance."

"Sorry. My mom scheduled me to fill in at one of the clubs tomorrow." Kelsey was glad to have other plans. She had enjoyed shopping for Patty's dress, but all the homecoming hype was beginning to get to her.

"Where is Jeremy taking you after the dance?" Patty asked Cheryl as part of her continued check on everyone's plans.

"He says it's going to be a surprise." Cheryl's shrug admitted she didn't know what to think about it.

"That sounds exciting," Barb said.

"Not necessarily. He could be taking you to the Hamburger Hut." Patty shook her finger in warning. "See if you can't get him to tell you what he has in mind."

"I'll try to find out tomorrow," Cheryl said gratefully.

"Everything seems to be going fine—except for you." Kelsey cringed. Patty peered at her. "Don't you want to go to the dance?"

"I never said I wouldn't go. I never said I didn't *want* to go. I like dressing up as much as anybody. And the band is going to be great."

"So why don't you get someone to ask you? You're cute. I'm sure a lot of guys would think about asking you out if they just knew you'd changed your mind about dating."

Kelsey had to smile at Patty's campaign to get her to the dance. "You mean I should pick someone and act impressed every time I'm around him?" she asked.

"That's a good start," Cheryl said with a nod.

"And then I should figure out how to sit by him at lunch, or better yet, I should get him to sit with us."

"I knew you still had it in you!" Patty exclaimed.

"Wrong," Kelsey told them emphatically. "I don't want a *date* for homecoming because it's too much stupid work to get one. If someone likes me enough to want to take me to the dance, he should be able to figure that out for himself!"

She expected them to argue, but the group fell silent. Then Kelsey noticed the shadow on the banner. Someone was standing behind her. Someone who left her friends speechless. She tilted her head backward and looked up.

"Hi, Shawn."

He smiled so broadly that his eyes crinkled. "Hi, Kelsey. Hey, you guys are doing a great job with that banner so far. I don't have anything on this afternoon, if you think you could use another painter."

"You want to paint with us?" Patty finally found her voice.

"Sure, if you'll let me," he answered, still looking at Kelsey.

"No one's painting the *A*," she told him, patting the empty space on the floor beside her.

"Good." He peeled off his leather jacket and knelt down next to her. Picking up a brush, he reached past Kelsey for the red paint. "Um, have you finished the popcorn puzzle yet?"

"Not yet," Kelsey answered self-consciously. No one else was saying a word. "You seemed to be the champion puzzler."

"I'd like to help you finish it." He spoke quietly so the others wouldn't hear him.

"That would be fun." She kept her voice low, too, but she knew her friends weren't missing a single word. She glanced covertly in their direction. All three were staring openly. Kelsey frowned at them, then realized that Shawn had followed her gaze.

Cheryl, Patty, and Barb looked quickly back down at the banner. Kelsey squirmed. Shawn touched her elbow. "Could I talk to you—alone—for a few minutes?"

"Sure." He probably had a few more questions about his history paper and was worried he might look dumb to her friends if he asked them. Talking about puzzles was bad enough. She started to stand. Shawn was already on his feet, and he put out a hand to help her. His hand around hers was warm and strong.

They walked outside the cafeteria and turned down a side hall. Kelsey suspected he was trying to put enough distance between them and her

49

friends to keep the girls from eavesdropping. He leaned against the wall with his hands in his pockets. Staring at the floor, he pretended to inspect his right shoe.

Kelsey waited patiently. She was stunned when he finally asked, "Would you like to go to homecoming with me?"

"Homecoming?" she asked. That was the last thing she had expected him to say. *He must have overheard us talking right before he came in,* she thought. He was probably asking her just because he felt sorry for her.

"I know you don't date," Shawn continued tentatively. "I thought we could go as friends."

"Friends." Once she got over her initial surprise, Kelsey realized the idea had possibilities. Shawn Horton was a nice person, his great looks aside. And he really sounded sincere about wanting her company at the dance.

"I'd like to go to hear the band and do some dancing, but I haven't spent enough time around school to know many people," Shawn concluded.

Kelsey hadn't thought about that. "I know what you mean. I'd like to see my friends all dressed up. I was thinking of going myself, but—"

"So what do you think? Why don't we go as two friends who couldn't find dates?"

Shawn Horton might be new at school, but Kelsey didn't believe he couldn't find a date. He must not have looked very hard. Still, his offer was tempting, and if she wanted to go with him, she knew she should say yes before he changed his mind.

"I'd like to go with you, Shawn."

"Then it's a deal!" He grinned and slapped her lightly on the shoulder. It was a gesture he might have used with a football buddy, but somehow it gave Kelsey a good feeling. Shawn just wanted to be with her, and that was nice.

He walked her back to her friends, but this time he didn't stop to help with the banner. Picking up his jacket, he said, "I'll call you later, Kelsey." He smiled over his shoulder as he walked away.

"Call you about what?"

"Did you see the look he gave you?"

"What did he want to talk about?"

Kelsey closed her eyes for a second, trying to prepare herself for the fuss her friends were going to make. No matter how she broke the news to them, they were going to go crazy.

"He asked me to go to homecoming with him—" All three girls screamed. She waited for the noise to die down before she finished. "He asked me to go as his *friend*."

"Don't worry about the *way* he asked you. The exact words aren't important. I'd go anywhere with Shawn Horton, even if he asked me to go as his *dog*," Cheryl said.

"You don't understand. I like it this way. I wouldn't have said yes if he'd asked me to be his *date*."

51

"That doesn't matter either," Patty said, ignoring Kelsey's sigh. "When can we get together? We have a lot of work to do on you, Kelsey Kramer, if you're going to be Shawn's date!"

"Really, guys. I don't need that much help."

"Sure you do," Cheryl and Barb insisted in unison.

"Thursday, at my house," Patty announced. "It will be our final strategy meeting. Who will be there?"

"Me," Cheryl said.

"I will, too," Barb added.

All eyes turned to Kelsey. If she didn't join them on Thursday, she might as well drop out of school. They would never forgive her. Resigned, she agreed, "Thursday, at Patty's."

Chapter Four

"Stop that!" Patty said, exasperated. "Why did you buy a strapless dress if you're going to tug at it all the time?"

Barb let go of her dress bodice and looked guilty. She smiled apologetically. "I thought it was falling."

"Trust me," Patty replied. "That dress is made to stay in place. It's not going to slip, but if it would make you feel better, we could attach it to your skin permanently—with Super Glue."

Kelsey laughed along with Cheryl. They were having a great time at the Thursday Homecoming Strategy Meeting in Patty's bedroom. Barb was the first to be analyzed by Patty, their recognized expert.

With her short auburn hair and fair skin, Barb looked great in the forest-green taffeta dress. The shiny, strapless top fit her perfectly, hugging her ribs, as it came to a *V* at the waist. The full skirt fell almost to her ankles and puffed out with the help of a stiff petticoat.

A few minutes earlier Cheryl had tried dancing with her, so they could see how the dress moved. When the skirt tangled in Cheryl's jean-covered legs, Kelsey had laughed so hard that she cried. Patty had hurried to demonstrate how far Barb must stay back from her partner to keep that from happening at the dance. Kelsey made a mental note to see how well Mark was dealing with Barb's skirt during the first slow dance.

"Now that you're done being Barb's date, you can put your dress on," Patty directed, and Cheryl obediently disappeared into an empty bedroom down the hall.

"How should I do my hair?" Barb asked.

Patty rubbed her chin with her hand while she studied Barb. "All those curls have to go. Too fluffy."

"A haircut?" Barb winced, putting a protective hand to her head.

"No. Just use some gel to smooth out the sides, and leave it fuller on the top." Patty stood behind Barb and pulled back the hair over each ear. "How does it look, Kelsey?"

"Super." She had to admit, Patty had an eye for style. The small change in Barb's hair turned her into something more than just a cute girl wearing a party dress—it gave her a total look.

"Good." Patty sounded satisfied.

"*Ooh*," Kelsey cried when Cheryl stepped back into Patty's bedroom. "You look like someone from *Gone with the Wind!*"

Kelsey leaned forward on the couch and hugged her knees, as Cheryl twirled. The white dress had enough ruffles and bows to transform her into a princess. It moved with every step she took. "The guys are going to die when they see you!" Barb exclaimed.

Kelsey wondered if she could find a dress that would make Shawn die, to use Barb's favorite phrase.

Patty pulled out a chair from the card table. "That dress is going to walk and dance just fine, but try sitting on it."

Cheryl sat in the chair and crossed her knees. One bare foot peeked out from under the dress.

"No, no, no," Patty scolded, rushing to Cheryl's side. "You're going to be Scarlett O'Hara at the dance. Would she have crossed her legs at the knee? Of course not!"

Cheryl uncrossed her legs and let Patty push her knees together and lean them to the right. Then Patty fussed with the ruffled skirt, fanning it out on both sides of the chair.

"*This* is how you sit in this dress," Patty announced.

Cheryl stood and walked to the far end of the room before she turned to face them. She held her arm out and bent it at the elbow as if she were holding someone's arm. "This dancin' has just exhausted me, Jeremy," she said in a bad southern drawl. "Could we set for a spell?" She fluttered her eyelashes outrageously at her unseen partner. When she got to her chair, she made a production of smoothing her skirt before she sat down. She then positioned her knees just the way Patty had shown her and arranged her skirt around her.

"How did I do?" Cheryl asked the group. Everyone was laughing too hard to answer. Still playing her part, Cheryl pouted and stamped her foot.

"I couldn't have done it better myself," Patty managed to say.

Cheryl smiled at the praise. They all knew Patty was the expert at the dating game.

"How are you going to fix your hair?" Patty asked, getting back down to business.

"I haven't decided. Do you have any ideas?"

"Do you remember how Scarlett O'Hara parted her hair in the middle and then pulled back her bangs and held them with bows?" All three of the other girls nodded. Cheryl used her fingers to comb through her hair and hold it back. "Tie them with little velvet ribbons and curl the rest of your hair," Patty instructed.

Kelsey nodded from her perch on the couch. Patty's advice was one-hundred-percent right.

"With your hair back, you'll need to do something spectacular with your eyes," Patty said.

"I'm wearing my regular shade of blue shadow," Cheryl told her.

"You always wear that shadow!" Patty nearly shouted. "Your homecoming date should be special. You can't wear your everyday face."

"But I don't know what else to do with this face!" Cheryl laughed for a minute before turning sober. "What could I do differently?"

"I'd use pinkish shadow and blue mascara," Patty replied with confidence. "I can lend you some of my makeup if you want to try it at home."

"Thank you—for everything," Cheryl said appreciatively.

"Yeah," Barb added. "You're a great friend."

Patty was amazing. Kelsey knew she was on top of every makeup and fashion trend, but that night she was a wizard. She had performed magic on Barb and Cheryl—they were going to look better than they could have imagined. Kelsey shifted on the couch, anxious for her turn.

"Want to see my outfit?" Patty asked them.

"Yes!" was the unanimous reply. She disappeared into the bedroom.

Barb's eyes sparkled with enthusiasm. "Can you believe how wonderful homecoming is going to be, thanks to Patty?"

"No kidding," Cheryl agreed. "I wouldn't have thought of half these details without her."

But would Cheryl's date really turn out any differently because of Patty's tips? Kelsey couldn't answer her own question. Where was the "dates-are-useless" Kelsey Kramer that night? Normally she would say that all Patty's guidance wouldn't change anything; dates either worked or they didn't. Mostly they didn't. Kelsey herself was living proof that a girl could know all the rules and still have rotten dates. But that night there was magic in the air, and she couldn't help feeling it.

Patty had convinced even Kelsey that homecoming wasn't like any other date. Kelsey was actually looking forward to spending the evening with Shawn. She had to admit it. She wanted to dress right and do her makeup in a special way that would make him think she was beautiful. She wanted him to look at her in a way that would make her melt in his arms when they danced.

Her heart raced at the thought. For the first time in weeks, she was sharing the excitement of dating fever with her friends. Thanks to Patty, homecoming just might be the exception to Kelsey's usual disastrous dating routine.

"How do you like this?" Patty asked, posing sideways in the bedroom door.

They groaned in envy. To put it simply, Patty could have stepped out of the pages of *Seventeen*. Her dusty-pink dress was strapless like Barb's, but the similarity ended there.

The entire bodice was shirred, and the folds in the shimmering fabric followed her curves, making her look incredibly sophisticated. The skirt fell in two levels, the first flaring out at midthigh, while the underskirt flounced a few inches past her knees. A saucy bow rested on her left hip. Her flat shoes were pink to match the dress, and her legs were covered by lacy white nylons.

Patty rocked on her heels, looking surprisingly nervous. "Say something, please."

"It's dynamite," Cheryl told her.

"The whole football team is going to fall over dead when they see you," Barb promised.

"You look fantastic." Kelsey's tone was lower and less enthusiastic. What kind of magic could Patty have left for *her*?

"My mom has a pearl necklace that I'm going to borrow." Patty's right hand traced across her neck, where the pearls would go. "And I'm having my hair done that morning. I think I'll have it all pulled to one side, and then let it fall over my shoulder in waves." She indicated one bare shoulder. "Oh, and I've been going to the tanning salon, so I won't look too pale. You should probably do that, too, Barb."

Kelsey sighed. Patty was still thinking of the others, even though it was her turn to gather compliments. She supposed Patty could afford to be generous because she already knew she was going to be gorgeous on homecoming night.

"And now it's time to talk about you." A determined gleam in her eyes, Patty turned to Kelsey.

Kelsey grinned, happy that Patty was finally ready to tell her what she would need to do to make her evening with Shawn work. Maybe it was too much to expect perfection, but Kelsey trusted her friends to help her make it a night to remember.

Patty was studying Kelsey. "I'm really busy this weekend, though. I don't think I'll have time to help you find a dress," she said finally, not sounding very disappointed.

"Are you sure?" Kelsey asked, realizing how much she really wanted Patty's advice.

"Sorry."

Patty's mood had changed, and Kelsey didn't know why. It was silly, but it hurt her feelings that Patty wasn't going to come with her. She didn't want the others to know she felt that way, though. "It's all right. My mom is so excited I'm going to the dance that she said she'd like to shop with me."

It was a lie. Her mother had been pleased because she thought Shawn was such a nice boy. Those were her very words. She had even extended curfew for homecoming night, but she hadn't said anything about shopping for a dress.

"Since I can't be with you, I thought we could check out some pictures." She pulled teen magazines from the shelf under the coffee table.

They huddled around the table, and Kelsey

felt her excitement building again. Patty turned the pages slowly, inspecting each advertisement hopefully. She paused a few times, but then she would shake her head and flip the page. Kelsey tried to imagine herself in some of the dresses, and it made her stomach tingle.

"What about this one?" Cheryl asked, pointing to a fluffy white gown much like her own.

"It's too frilly. A dress like that is fine for you, Cheryl, but Shawn's too mature for his date to be dressed like that."

Kelsey opened her mouth to disagree, but Patty's words sounded final. She was right about Shawn seeming more grown-up than most of the other guys at Spring Hill High, but did that mean she'd have to dress like she was thirty?

"Then this one," Barb suggested when a slinky black dress appeared two pages later.

"I don't think so," Kelsey told them, knowing her body hadn't been built for plunging necklines.

"I agree," Patty said, ending all doubts. "Shawn might be that sophisticated, but Kelsey isn't."

It struck Kelsey that she didn't like Patty's attitude. Suddenly she seemed to be an expert on Shawn Horton. "How do you know so much about what Shawn likes and what he thinks?"

"I don't know from personal experience with Shawn, but I *have* dated guys like him before. Remember T.J.?"

Who wouldn't remember T.J., Patty's date for the spring prom? Kelsey thought, raising an eyebrow at Barb and Cheryl. He had been a rich senior who seemed more interested in expensive cars and designer clothes than in high school. Classes and sports bored him, or at least that was what he wanted people to believe. Patty had schemed overtime to keep him interested in her, but he had dumped her for a college girl during the summer. Patty had been heartbroken, but Kelsey figured it was the best thing that could have happened. She had always thought T.J. was a phony.

"Well, if you think Shawn is as hot as T.J., why didn't you get him to ask *you* to homecoming?" Kelsey's question seemed to startle everyone, but she was suddenly wondering why Patty had settled for the captain of the football team.

"I learned my lesson with T.J.," Patty admitted, her voice quiet and serious. "To tell you the truth, Kelsey, Shawn Horton is out of my league. Guys like him have different rules, and I don't know them."

Kelsey felt her stomach falling. Patty's dating rules were the only ones she knew. If they didn't apply to Shawn, how was she ever going to survive homecoming? If Patty couldn't tell her how to dress or how to fix her hair, then how was she supposed to figure it out on her own?

"Want to see something?" Patty asked, pulling a scrapbook from under the table. She spread it open to reveal newspaper photos. Photos of Shawn.

Kelsey's mouth fell open as she studied the photographs. He looked so serious in most of the shots, his jaw locked, his mouth unsmiling. His eyes were the only part of his face that seemed alive. They looked out from the photographs and challenged the newspaper readers to buy the clothes he was wearing.

She recognized his expressions as typical model poses, but she was shocked at how different he looked from the Shawn she knew. Where was the smile? Where was the sparkle in his eyes that told her he enjoyed being with her? The guy in these pictures was someone else, a guy she had no right to know. Maybe Patty was right. Maybe Shawn was another T.J. in disguise.

"Here's my favorite." Patty turned the page with a flick of her wrist, and all four of them gasped.

It was Shawn in a loose-knit fisherman's sweater, his arm resting on a girl's shoulder. She was only as tall as his chin, and the picture showed him in profile looking down into her upturned face. They both had flushed cheeks, as if they had just come inside from a romp in the snow. The broad smile on his face made his eyes crinkle at the corners, and his hair had fallen over his forehead.

"Don't you wish you could be her?" Cheryl whispered.

"I would die, honestly," Barb said.

"What are you going to do if he smiles at you that way?" Patty asked, the only practical one in the group.

Kelsey smiled, thinking of the honest emotions she'd seen in Shawn's eyes and the wonderful feeling it always gave her when he smiled. That very smile from the advertisement was one of the things that had convinced her to trust him. Shawn was no T.J.

"I'd smile back." She knew Patty would flutter her eyelashes and say something so sugary Shawn would choke. Maybe Patty had been right about her rules not working with him.

"You can't turn a sappy smile on a guy like Shawn and expect him to take you seriously."

"Don't knock it unless you've tried it," Kelsey said softly.

The knots in her stomach were unraveling, as she realized Patty had the wrong idea about Shawn and her. First, Shawn was not a conceited jerk like T.J. And second, Shawn was not Kelsey's date, he was her friend. Remembering how comfortable she felt being around Shawn, she knew she wouldn't want it any other way.

"You are so lucky, Kelsey." Patty closed the scrapbook, with a sigh of admiration. "I'd give anything for a chance to land a guy like Shawn."

"You make him sound like a fish!" The girls giggled. Kelsey crossed her arms and leaned back into the sofa. "I don't want to *land* Shawn, I just want to spend some time with him."

Chapter Five

"I think you'll like it here." Jill offered a friendly smile as the two of them slipped into a booth at Granny's Kitchen.

"Everything sure smells good." Kelsey opened the menu to find a list of soups and sandwiches that all sounded delicious. Jill had invited her to lunch so they could "get to know each other better."

They read their menus in silence. Kelsey knew she wanted a turkey sandwich. She could set her menu down on the table, but then she wouldn't know what to do next. She and Jill had chatted comfortably in the car, but Kelsey couldn't think of anything more to say to her.

Jill folded her menu and gave their orders to the waitress. After she left, Jill cleared her throat and said, "Well, it's nice to finally be getting a sister. I've waited all my life for this."

"Really?"

"Seriously," Jill assured her. "All I ever had was a rotten older brother. I longed to have a sister when I was growing up."

"I know what you mean—about brothers and about wanting a sister." Kelsey blushed when she realized one of the rotten brothers she was talking about was the man Jill was going to marry.

"My brother was never exactly nice to me, but he *really* got mean after the time I turned the garden hose on him when he was kissing some girl on the front step." Jill smiled mischievously.

Kelsey laughed out loud. She couldn't imagine Jill, the poised woman with perfect manners, pulling such a prank. "You didn't really do that!"

"Yes, I did. I heard that you did about the same thing once." Jill smiled, and Kelsey knew Eric must have told her about the one time she got revenge on him.

"I didn't spray him with the hose. I rigged up a bucket on top of the door so it fell on him as he left to pick up his date for the prom."

"What was his date like?" Jill asked, her eyes twinkling.

"She was really pretty." Kelsey remembered wondering why someone like her would date Eric.

"Then maybe I should thank you for ruining his date with her!" Jill said with a laugh.

The jokes put Kelsey at ease, and she felt like the time was right to talk to Jill about her brother. "Do you love Eric?" She blushed at the boldness of her question.

Jill's eyes widened in surprise. "Of course I do. I'm going to marry him in two months."

"I know that." Kelsey bit her lip. She didn't want to be rude, but on the other hand, she really wanted to understand what Jill felt for Eric. "I guess what I meant was *how* can you love a guy like him?"

Jill sank back against the cushion at the back of the booth. "Would you like me to tell you about it?"

"Yes, please. I'd like to know how it happened."

Jill rested her hands on the table and began to speak. "My junior year of college, Eric was dating my best friend. The three of us spent a lot of time together. Somehow Eric and I got to be friends—"

"That's hard to believe," Kelsey interrupted. A friend was someone you could trust, and she had never been able to trust her older brother.

"I didn't expect it to happen," Jill said, "but I felt comfortable with Eric. I found myself telling him things I hadn't told my girlfriends. It was great having a friend like him—until he started to tease me."

"I know the feeling." Kelsey shook her head grimly. "I told him all about this awful date I had once, and he mentioned that guy every time he saw me for the next month. How could you stand him being so mean?"

"Did you ever think he might not be doing it to be mean?"

Kelsey was confused. "Of course he did it to be mean! What other reason could he have had?"

Jill tilted her head thoughtfully to one side. "When my friend and Eric stopped dating, he asked me out. Before I could get involved with him, we had a long talk about his habit of turning everything into a joke. And do you know what I discovered?"

"I haven't the slightest idea." *This ought to be good,* Kelsey told herself.

"Eric is very uncomfortable in serious situations. He hates to see people unhappy. He doesn't deal well with other people's problems. Instead of worrying, he automatically tries to lighten situations with jokes."

"Are you saying all his Rick-the-Rat jokes were supposed to make me feel better?" Eric had really missed the mark if that was his intent. He had just added to her problems.

"Maybe . . ." Jill hesitated. "Or, maybe he was paying you back for dumping water on him when he was ready to take some gorgeous girl to the prom."

Kelsey got the point and laughed. Jill really understood Eric. "But did you really solve your problem with Eric? I've seen him laughing at you sometimes."

"He still teases me, but not in ways that hurt me. He wouldn't be the man I fell in love with if he stopped joking around." Kelsey raised her eyebrows, wondering how that could be true, and Jill explained further. "I was too serious about life when I met Eric. He has helped me loosen up and enjoy myself more." Jill leaned across the table toward Kelsey with a confiding smile. "Love is a funny thing. It changes the people involved—you share your strengths, you improve on your weaknesses, you respect each other, you help each other, you dream together."

"That sounds nice. . . ." Kelsey was startled to find herself thinking that love sounded like *fun.* Jill's world of love was so different from Patty's world of games and rules.

"What about *your* experiences with men?" Jill asked without a trace of laughter in her words. Kelsey felt like they were two adults discussing the men in their lives. "Weren't you dating a redheaded boy early last summer before you visited your aunt in Wisconsin and got involved there, too?"

"My disaster in Wisconsin was not a romance." Kelsey still shuddered to think about it, even two and a half months later. "Rick was a certified rat. He seemed considerate, thoughtful, and fun. We were inseparable for a week—until his girlfriend came back—the girlfriend I didn't even know existed. She dropped by a party Rick had taken me to, and the next thing I knew, I didn't have a ride home."

Jill pursed her lips. "You're right to call him a rat, but what about the redhead? I saw him once at your house. He looked like a regular guy."

"I guess you didn't look closely enough." Kelsey giggled. "That was Jon Rossiter. We went out a few times, but all he wanted to do was laugh at everything. He loved to make fun of other people. Once at the mall he put a ketchup pack in his shirt and pretended he was bleeding to death. He was always looking for ways to make me look foolish."

"He doesn't sound very sensitive," Jill allowed. "Did you ever tell him that his constant jokes bothered you?"

Kelsey's mouth fell open. Why would she have done that? "No. Never."

"Why does the idea shock you? I had to tell Eric that I didn't like certain things about him before we could work through our problems."

"But, Jill, it's not in the rules. I mean, it's not *done*." Kelsey was nearly speechless.

"What rules?" Jill inquired, shaking her head. Now she was the one who seemed confused. "Or should I say *whose* rules?"

"My friend Patty knows how to handle guys. She helps the rest of us know how to act."

"What are some of these rules?" Jill really sounded curious.

"The regular stuff, you know. If you dress right and say the right things, guys will like you." Jill raised an eyebrow, and Kelsey felt that she had to continue. "You talk about their interests, you have to like their friends, and you never bore them with problems of your own—"

"What do you, or Patty, get in return?"

"Dates, obviously," Kelsey told her. That was the dumbest question she had ever heard.

"Dates with guys like Rick and Jon?"

Kelsey expected to see a grin on Jill's face, but her almost-sister-in-law was completely serious. "Patty gets good dates. I only had bad ones because I didn't know all the rules, or else I wasn't using them right."

"You don't sound like someone who has given up dating," Jill said gently.

"Well, I have. Guys are strange people, Jill. I don't know how to deal with a guy if the rules don't work. I just decided it's easier to quit playing the game for a while."

"I can see your point." Jill stopped while the waitress put down her chef's salad and Kelsey's sandwich. "But there's something you're not realizing. There are all kinds of men in the world—some are rats, some are too good to be true, and most are somewhere in between. How can you expect to treat all of these *people* the same way, using one set of rules?"

"I don't know, but what else is there to do?" Kelsey didn't have any idea of how to interact with the male half of the world without Patty's instructions.

"Men are people, too, Kelsey. Treat them as you'd treat any friend."

"Maybe that works with older men, but I'm talking about high school boys!"

"You could be right. It's been a few years since I've dealt with high school boys. All I know is that Eric and I were friends before we ever fell in love, and it worked for us." Jill shrugged as if romance were still a mystery to her, too.

"Could I ask a favor?" Kelsey ventured shyly when Jill paused.

"Sure, we're sisters, almost." She winked and Kelsey winked back.

"I was wondering if you would help me shop for my homecoming dress."

Jill smiled broadly. "I'd love to!"

"It's not really a big deal. Shawn and I are just going as friends." She didn't want Jill to get carried away as Patty and the others had.

"There's nothing wrong with going out with a friend. Look where it got me," Jill said, flashing her diamond engagement ring in Kelsey's direction.

The switch on the hair dryer made a dull click, but nothing else happened. "*Tommy-y-y!*"

Kelsey's wail echoed down the hall, and shuffling footsteps came from the direction of Tommy's bedroom. Her brother peeked around the corner. "What's wrong?"

"By any chance did you *fix* the hair dryer

lately?" The dead blower was hanging limply from her hand. The only thing that looked more pathetic was her wet hair, but she couldn't see that very well in the foggy mirror.

"I took it apart last night—"

"Why?" she asked from between gritted teeth.

"To see how it worked."

"You couldn't have learned much. I'd bet money this thing will never work again!"

"Sorry," he said in a small voice.

"What good is that? Shawn is picking me up in less than two hours, and my hair is going to dry into a flat mop! Why did I ever have to have a brother like you, anyway?"

The door was pushed open a little farther, and Jill's head appeared in the bathroom. "Could I help you?"

"Only if you have a hair dryer in your purse." Kelsey threw her brush into the sink, but it didn't make her feel any better.

"I could run home and bring mine over," she offered.

"Jill," came Eric's annoyed whisper from the hall. "We're meeting them in a few minutes."

Jill's head disappeared from the bathroom. "It won't take long." Jill's voice was calm, but firm.

"At least fifteen minutes," he argued.

"But it's important—this is her homecoming." It got too quiet, and Kelsey figured Jill was cuddling up to her brother. She had noticed that happening before.

"OK," he finally said. "After all, she's doing it for a good guy. I like Shawn."

Fifteen minutes. That would give her time to do her makeup. Forcing a determined smile, Kelsey wrapped her hair in a towel and promised herself she wouldn't worry about it.

Luckily her father had been able to repair the radio that Tommy had attacked. She turned it up louder and snapped her fingers to the music while she waited for the mirror to clear. As soon as she could see her face, Kelsey was humming and applying her mascara.

"*Ow!*" Next to not having a hair dryer, stabbing the mascara wand in her eye was the worst thing she could have done. Her eye was stinging, and there was a brown smear under it. "If anything else goes wrong, this is going to seem like a real date."

She recognized the familiar feeling of dread in the bottom of her stomach. It had to stop. There was no reason to be tense. She and Shawn were going to the dance as *friends*. He wasn't expecting her to be an eyelash-fluttering princess. She didn't have to smile at all his jokes and worry about making entertaining conversation. Taking two deep breaths, she whispered, "Relax, Kelsey Kramer."

A sudden commotion outside the bathroom told her Jill had returned. At the knock on the door, Kelsey welcomed her inside.

Jill uncoiled the cord that was wrapped around the dryer. "How are you going to fix your hair?"

"Nothing special. I'm just planning to curl the ends under." If Shawn had liked her in her glasses and a sweat suit, then she didn't need a celebrity hairstyle for the dance.

"I found something at home that I thought would look perfect with your dress." Jill took a pearl necklace and matching bracelet from her pocket and handed them to Kelsey.

She reached for them, catching the strands in her fingers. Their rich, lustrous sheen took Kelsey's breath away. "They're beautiful," she whispered.

"My parents gave the set to me when I graduated from high school."

"And you don't mind lending them to me?"

Jill smiled. "I know you'll take care of them, and besides, what good are they sitting in my jewelry box?"

"Well, thanks." Kelsey put the necklace around her neck and fastened the clasp.

"I think it will look better with your dress," Jill teased. Kelsey checked her reflection in the mirror and agreed her fitted bathrobe didn't do the necklace justice.

"Honey," Eric called impatiently from the hall.

Jill rolled her eyes at the sound of Eric's voice and then turned back to Kelsey. "If you don't need any more help, I guess I'll be going."

"I'll be just fine," she said, flipping on the dryer.

Jill hesitated at the door for a few seconds before she threw her arms around Kelsey. "Just be yourself tonight and have a good time."

Kelsey was still smiling when the door closed behind Jill. Although her friends had some terrible stories about life with their sisters, she thought it felt good to have a woman closer to her own age in the family. Maybe Jill and Eric were one case of a romance that worked.

Setting her hair on hot rollers, she let her thoughts drift back to the homecoming game earlier that afternoon. She had gone with Patty, and they had sat with Cheryl and Barb and their dates. Patty's homecoming date, Cliff, was on the field leading the Spring Hill Tigers to victory. Shawn had to work, and Kelsey was surprised how much she had missed him when the other girls were sitting in the stands with their boyfriends. Not that he was a potential boyfriend, but she would have liked sharing the game with him all the same.

With her hair off her face in the rollers, she made another attempt at her makeup. This time there were no incidents. The mascara made her eyelashes look longer. Her pastel shadow and shimmering blush gave her face a glamorous look. She shook her hair out once the rollers were back in their case.

"Not bad, Kramer," she told herself as she

viewed her bouncy curls and finished face. O
course her old robe didn't add much to th
image. It was time for phase two: the dress.

"Let me help you," her mother offered when
she stepped into the hall. They walked to he
bedroom, where the pale lilac dress had been
laid across the bed.

"I need some help," Kelsey admitted, shrug
ging out of her robe. Like her friends, it would
only be the second or third time she had worn a
formal dress. She bet they would all get butter
flies when they looked at themselves in thei
mirrors—even Patty. Kelsey knew she'd have
trouble getting into her dress by herself.

"You're going to look so pretty tonight," he
mother promised, as Kelsey stepped into th
dress. When she turned slowly to model he
outfit, her mom sighed. "You look wonderful
sweetheart."

It was an off-the-shoulder dress with a ruffl
that flounced across her shoulders at an angle
covering just the top of her arms. And the skir
was full, with a row of ruffles at the hem.

"Want to use my mirror?" Mrs. Kramer asked

"Definitely." They moved to her parents' bed
room, and Kelsey posed in front of the full
length mirror on the back of the door. Sh
glanced from her shoulders to her feet and ther
back to her neck, where the pearls shone. "Thi
is great!"

"Shawn should be here in about ten min

ites," her mother said, checking the clock on he nightstand. "What do you still need to do?"

"Find my shoes, finish my hair, and put on some lipstick." Kelsey counted off the items on her fingers.

"I'll get your shoes while you do the rest."

Back in the bathroom, Kelsey looked at her hair. It was full and bouncy, but nothing special. She tried combing one side up and back and clipping it in place. Patty wore her hair that way sometimes, but it made Kelsey look lopsided.

"I give up," she told the mirror, just as the doorbell rang. It had to be Shawn. She shook her hair back into place and fluffed her bangs. It wasn't spectacular, but her hair was fuller and curlier than usual. It would have to do.

There was a soft knock on the bathroom door. "Shawn is here," her mother said. "Your shoes are outside the door."

"I'll be right down." She ran some frosty pink lipstick over her lips and took a deep breath. Knowing she couldn't hide in the bathroom all night, she opened the door, stepped into her shoes, and started down to the living room.

She didn't get far. Her feet turned to lead, and her heart did a backflip. Shawn Horton looked phenomenal.

It wasn't just the black tux, the white shirt with pleats in the front, or his matching gray cummerbund and bow tie, or even the way he stood with one hand casually resting in his pants pocket. It was the total picture. Kelsey told herself it was just his model's training, but she couldn't believe any other guy at the dance was going to look this good. She remembered Cheryl's date complaining about renting a "monkey suit," and she bet he *would* look like a monkey in his tux compared to Shawn.

"You look great!" he said, looking up at Kelsey on the stairs.

"Thanks. So do you." Her feet were slowly moving again, and she made it all the way down the stairs.

He reached for a box that he had set on the hall table while he was waiting for her. She knew it contained a corsage, and it suddenly hit her that he was going to try to pin it on her dress. How was he going to do that when her neck and shoulders were nearly bare?

"I'm glad you told me what color your dress was. I think this will look good with it." He opened the box, and Kelsey peeked inside.

An orchid! It was perfect. Shawn lifted the flower out of the box. Kelsey glanced down at her dress doubtfully.

"Hold out your arm," he instructed.

Her arm? She stretched her left hand toward him. Then she saw the elastic band at the base of the flower, and its lilac ribbon. Her worries had been for nothing; it was a wrist corsage.

Shawn seemed to know how to do everything right.

"I've got something for you, too," she said, remembering the boutonniere she had been keeping fresh in the refrigerator. She hurried to the kitchen, but her mother was already there, waiting with the package in her hand. Kelsey unwrapped the single rose and returned to Shawn.

"A boutonniere for a friend?" he teased when she raised up on her toes to fasten the flower to his lapel with a stick pin.

"Why not? Look what you did for me!" She lifted her arm showing off her orchid.

"Mmm . . ." He grinned. "I guess we're a good pair."

She bit her lip, knowing she was ruining her lipstick, but she couldn't help it. His eyes were shining down on her in admiration, just as she had dreamed they might the other night at Paty's house.

"Are you ready to go?" he asked as he held her coat for her. And when he offered her his arm, she said, "I'm as ready as I'll ever be."

He smiled. "Then let's do it!"

Chapter Six

The dance had already started when they arrived. Shawn took her coat and left it at the coat check. Then they headed for the cafeteria. Shawn started into the room, but Kelsey held back. She just wanted to get a good look at the decorations and the crowd, or so she told herself.

"Can we wait just a minute?" she asked.

He came back to stand next to her. "Nervous?"

She nodded. It felt strange to be going to the dance with someone who wasn't her date. Not that she wished Shawn *were* her date, she just wasn't sure how she was supposed to act.

"The band sounds good," Shawn said idly.

The band was playing at the far end of the cafeteria. The long lunch tables had disappeared for the evening. Streamers hung from the ceiling, waving gently above their heads as a breeze blew through the room from an open window. The night air was cool, but it was refreshing in the warm room.

"Hey, Horton," called a big guy moving toward them. Kelsey recognized him as Ralph, a football player. He slapped Shawn on the back and then peered at her. "Is it really Kelsey Kramer?"

She had expected some of the girls to be amazed that she was at the dance with Shawn, but it hadn't crossed her mind that the guys might be surprised to see her there as well.

"I thought you had quit dating," he said to Kelsey.

Before she could launch into an explanation of her friendship with Shawn, her partner answered for her. "It was just a matter of asking her the right way."

Her head snapped toward Shawn. He made it sound as if he didn't take her nondating decision seriously—as if she had merely been waiting for the right boy to change her mind. She couldn't believe it!

Kelsey's mouth started to open to argue with him when Shawn squeezed her hand. As soon as their visitor left them to find his date, Shawn leaned down to whisper in her ear. "I didn't mean to upset you. But Ralph isn't too smart. He wouldn't have understood the real story."

The fact that Ralph barely managed to pass his classes was well known around Spring Hill High. Kelsey had to laugh at the idea of trying to explain her relationship with Shawn to him. "You're right."

His hand touched her left elbow. "Would you like to dance?"

She had been looking for her friends to say "hi," but no one was in sight. So dancing sounded like a great idea. The band was playing a good song, and she was ready to start having fun. She flashed him a grin. "I'd love to."

He led her to a spot close to the band. When they started dancing, Kelsey realized she wasn't the only one admiring Shawn's style and grace. Girls were ignoring their own dates to watch him. Others were craning their necks to discover who was lucky enough to be Shawn's partner.

When his right hand reached out for hers, Kelsey honestly felt the tension around her. It was hard to believe the girls could be jealous of her. They had to know there was nothing heavy between her and Shawn. Still, Kelsey had to admit she was very happy to be with him that night.

They locked hands but kept their bodies at arms' length until the song was over. After the song ended, Shawn tugged firmly on her hand to pull her toward him. She felt her face growing warm, while her knees turned to jelly.

He slipped his left arm around her waist and then released her hand. She took a deep breath as the fingers on his free hand slipped under her necklace. The feel of his slightly rough fingers against her skin made her shiver. She looked up to find a smile on his face that reached to his sparkling eyes.

"What's a girl who doesn't believe in romance doing with feminine ruffles on her dress and pearls around her neck?"

She laughed self-consciously. It was a good question. "Jill lent the necklace to me. She's very romantic these days—with the wedding and all. It's pretty, isn't it?"

"Yes, it is." He let the pearls drop back against her throat, and his hand traced across her collarbone, until he brushed her hair over her shoulder.

The band started another fast song. Relieved, Kelsey moved back a few steps, so they could dance without getting tangled together. Someone grabbed her arm from behind, and she turned around to discover Patty.

"Looks pretty cozy," her friend whispered with a knowing glint in her dark eyes. When Kelsey just shrugged, Patty continued, "I saw him whispering to you when you snuggled up to him."

"Give me a break!" Kelsey sounded more casual than she felt. She really didn't want people to think that was what they had been doing.

Patty's date joined them, but before leaving with him, she bent close to Kelsey. "Bet you can't wait for a slow dance!"

Although Kelsey had been looking forward to

dancing in Shawn's arms when she had thought about homecoming before, Patty's tone flustered her. Her friend made it sound as if she were putting the moves on Shawn, and that just wasn't true. Sure, she liked to be close to him. But now she was worried. Was she supposed to want to slow dance with a *friend?*

She didn't have time to debate it. The next song was a tender ballad, and Shawn reached out for her. Before he could get his arm around her waist, she said the first thing that came into her head. "You know, I'm really thirsty."

"Thirsty? After two dances?"

She put her hand on her throat and faked a cough. "I've just dried up. Could we get some punch?"

"Sure. I wouldn't want my friend fainting or anything."

"Thanks," she mumbled sheepishly.

They zigzagged through the dancers until they reached the long table set up just inside the cafeteria doors. Parent volunteers were pouring soft drinks and ladling punch from the large bowl.

"Two punches," Shawn requested. He took both cups and looked down at Kelsey. "Let's sit at one of those little tables."

Kelsey led the way to the edge of the room where intimate tables had been set up for tired dancers. Some tables had hurricane lamps, but she chose one with a bouquet of balloons as its centerpiece. Shawn set the punch down and pulled out Kelsey's chair. After she was seated, he moved his chair close to hers.

She sipped the punch and realized her problem wasn't solved yet. It was a very small glass, and it wasn't going to last for the whole dance, unless she drank slowly. After a second sip, she set her cup back on the table.

"You're not drinking much, for someone who was dying of thirst a few minutes ago," Shawn observed.

"Just trying to be a lady," Kelsey replied, remembering all the times her mother had said it was unbecoming to chug a glass of milk or soda.

Shawn cocked his head and pretended to study her. "I guess you're doing a pretty good job of that."

She brought the cup to her lips again to hide her smile. If he only knew what she'd gone through to look like a lady for him! "You'll never guess what Tommy did today," she said.

"He blew all the fuses at your house." He scooted even closer to her and rested his arm on the back of her chair.

"Almost that bad! He took the hair dryer apart to see how it worked."

"And he had a few pieces left over, the way he did with his race car?"

"No. This time he put everything back inside, but the results weren't any better. Less than three hours ago, I was standing in my bathroom with hopelessly wet hair. I thought I was going to look like a sheep dog tonight!"

He laughed at the picture. "Obviously someone fixed it, because you're no dog," he retorted.

She hung her head, pretending to be embarrassed by his compliment. "Thanks. But really, Jill had to lend me her hair dryer."

His hand reached up from her back and tangled in her hair. "I like whatever you did with it. Some of the girls here are wearing more hairspray than clothes!" He glanced out at the crowd, and Kelsey would have sworn he looked right at Patty.

She shook her head so her waves flew freely. "You like the windblown look better?"

His grin showed his perfect teeth. "I like you because you're so natural. Modeling is all make-believe. I have much more fun with you."

Kelsey felt warm inside as if she'd just taken a big gulp of hot chocolate. Shawn Horton preferred her to models with bodies and clothes that any girl would envy? She flushed with pleasure.

Gazing at the dancers, she suddenly found Barb and Mark. It looked like Barb was following Patty's advice faithfully, holding herself far enough away from Mark so her stiff skirt didn't trip him. Even more amazing—Barb's top was staying in place without tugs or adjustments. Maybe she really had used Super Glue!

"What are you smiling about?"

"Smiling?" Kelsey realized she had been grinning at Barb and Mark without knowing it. "I'm just enjoying myself."

The song ended, and Kelsey saw Patty heading toward the refreshment table. She swallowed the rest of her punch and pushed away her glass. If she huddled there with Shawn much longer, it would give Patty more ideas.

"Finished?" He helped her out of her chair, and they started back to the dance floor.

She saw Cheryl and her date walking hand in hand to the punch table. Her friend really did look beautiful, and Patty's suggestions were working perfectly. Cheryl was floating across the floor in her white dress, and her hair looked great pulled back with velvet ribbons. Jeremy was fussing over her as if she were Scarlett O'Hara herself.

"Now what's so interesting?" Shawn asked, trying to follow her gaze.

"Was I smiling again?"

"No. You were just concentrating on something so hard that you didn't hear what I said to you." Shawn tried to sound gruff, but she didn't believe he was angry.

"Sorry. I was thinking how nice Cheryl looks."

"That's a relief." His arm slipped around her waist. "I was worried you'd found some other guy you'd rather be with tonight."

"I'm sure, Horton." She knew he couldn't be

serious. "What did you try to tell me when I wasn't listening?"

"I just asked if you're having a good time." The light tone was gone from his voice, and Kelsey knew he wanted an honest answer this time.

Ignoring her common sense, which told her she was not acting as just a friend, she rested her head on his shoulder. "I'm having a great time. And don't worry that I'm looking around for a different escort. I wouldn't want to be here with anyone else."

"Spoken like a true friend." He hugged her against him. "Let's dance some more."

By the time the band began another slow song, Kelsey was truly tired. She and Shawn had danced for at least half an hour without resting. When she heard the band harmonizing on the opening bars, she took Shawn's hand and tugged on it.

"Can't we sit down for a little while?" she pleaded, still trying to catch her breath.

Shawn stood his ground. "You don't want to slow dance with me, do you? I'm not going to hurt you, Kelsey."

She looked at the floor and fought the blush that was rising on her cheeks. He was making her feel foolish. How could she explain her hesitancy? Shawn probably thought she didn't like him that much or that she was embarrassed to be seen dancing with him.

His hand slid under her chin, and he tipped her head back so she couldn't avoid his eyes. "What's wrong, Kelsey?"

"We're friends," she whispered, moving closer so no one else would hear their conversation.

"Good friends," he agreed.

"Do *good friends* do this sort of thing?"

An easy smile spread across his face as he finally understood her problem. "Friends like us should."

His right arm circled her waist. His other hand captured hers, and there was nothing for her to do except rest her free hand on his shoulder and start moving her feet. The wrist corsage was next to her face, and she hid her eyes behind its petals.

"Relax," Shawn whispered into her hair.

Kelsey couldn't relax. Shawn's hand was too warm on her back. She had three choices: She could stare at his chest, look up into his face, or check out the people around them. The last choice sounded more interesting than the first and safer than the second.

Gazing past Shawn's shoulder, she saw Patty and Cliff. She smiled at Patty, but her best friend was oblivious of everyone but the captain of the football team.

Barb and Mark were dancing close to the other couple. He was holding her gently, and Kelsey suspected he wouldn't eat all the popcorn on a movie date with Barb. It was funny the way things had turned out for the best, she decided. If Mark had been nicer to her, then she wouldn't have given up dating, and she wouldn't be at the homecoming dance with Shawn, a friend.

"Are you having a good time?" he asked softly.

"Yes. Are you?"

His answer was a deep sigh. Kelsey forgot her cautionary measures and looked up at him. There was just the smallest smile on his lips, and his eyes saw only her. This was what she had dreamed about during the strategy meeting. And this was better than being the girl in the advertisement, because this was real. Being so close to him made her heart beat out a crazy rhythm.

Shawn had been right. Friends should dance together. Kelsey sighed and laid her head against him, closing her eyes. As she relaxed, Shawn rested his chin on the top of her head. She had never felt like that with a guy before—that happy, that wanted, that safe.

Thinking about how anxious the girls at school had been the past few weeks and how happy they all looked tonight, Kelsey realized that she was feeling a different kind of excitement. She was having a wonderful time, but she didn't feel that nervous energy that went with dating. Instead, she was enjoying being comfortable with Shawn, a guy whom half the girls would have gladly given up their dates for.

*　　*　　*

Kelsey set her fork on her empty salad plate and looked across the table at Shawn. The candle made shadows on his face. A bouquet of flowers had stood in the center of the table, but he moved it to one side, saying he hadn't brought her to an expensive restaurant to peek at her through leaves and stems.

"It's good to know I've been right about dating," she said.

"Why do you say that?" It sounded like a casual question. He chased the last pieces of lettuce across his plate.

"Because I've had more fun tonight than I've ever had on a *date*," she said triumphantly.

"Maybe it was the company," he challenged.

"No. It was because I was out with a friend, not with a date." It made perfect sense to Kelsey.

"I see it another way," Shawn said, looking directly at her, and Kelsey wondered why she felt nervous. Her answer came when he continued, "We're having a good time together. It shouldn't matter if we call it a date."

"Are you saying we're on a date?" Her voice cracked. To avoid looking at him she concentrated on twisting the napkin in her lap.

"It kind of seems like it," he answered.

Kelsey felt like a fool. Shawn had invited her to homecoming, bought her a corsage, and danced with only her all night. *Friends* might have gone together and left together, but they would have been on their own during the dance itself. But then again, she had told Shawn the story about the hair-dryer crisis, not a story she would ordinarily share with a date. But then again . . .

Why had she let herself believe they were going as friends? Kelsey didn't have an exact answer, but she knew it had something to do with the way Shawn looked at her and the way she felt when she was with him.

Suddenly Kelsey realized she was squirming in her seat, trying to make her dress rub against her itching stomach. Her stomach was itching? That was a bad sign.

"Do you think the salad dressing had any garlic in it?" she asked slowly, dreading his answer.

He made a face, and Kelsey knew he was wondering how the conversation had jumped from dating to salad dressing. "We both had the house dressing. I can ask if it had garlic in it, if it'll help you."

"Don't bother," she said unhappily. "I know it did."

"How?"

"I'm allergic to it."

Worry put a crease between his eyebrows. "Are you going to start wheezing or something?"

"No. I just get hives." She hugged her arms around her waist, hoping the pressure would reduce the itching.

"Are you sure? I don't see any. Maybe there wasn't any garlic—"

"They're on my stomach, and I'm itching to death."

"Should we leave?" He really looked confused. It was probably the first time a girl had gotten hives with him.

"Let's stay for dinner. It's time you learned what it's like to be on a date with Kelsey Kramer. I promise you'll find out why I gave it up."

"Quit being so silly. We've had a good time so far, and—"

The waitress appeared with one plate, and she set it in front of Shawn. "Miss, did you order the fish?"

"Yes, I did."

"I'm so sorry, but the chef lost the order. I'll have him put your fish under the broiler immediately. We apologize for the inconvenience." She turned to smile at Shawn. "And, sir, you won't be charged for the lady's meal."

"Wonderful," Kelsey grumbled under her breath. The missing dinner wasn't a very big surprise. It was the kind of thing she expected to have happen on dates. Now she could sit in her chair, scratch her hives, and watch Shawn eat his steak. So much for having a good time.

"This is terrible," Shawn said. "Do you want to share my dinner?" He started to cut a chunk off his steak.

"No. I'll wait for my fish." She stopped herself

before she added, "If I'd wanted steak, I would have ordered it."

"At least have part of my potato. Then I'll take half of yours when it comes." He sawed his baked potato in half and put one part on his bread and butter plate.

Kelsey accepted the plate when he handed it across the table. She dropped a pat of butter on her potato and sat back to let it melt. There was no reason for her to hurry.

"I don't want you to think everything is turning bad just because I called this a date," Shawn said while he cut into his steak.

"Are you saying it's not surprising for your dates to break out in hives and have their dinner orders disappear?" asked Kelsey grimly.

Shawn choked back a laugh. "No, in all honesty, Kelsey, no one has ever had an allergic reaction on me before."

She held her head high, as if to say "I told you so."

"But it doesn't mean you're right. There's a first time for everything," he protested.

What an optimist, she thought, sinking her fork into the potato. She couldn't help wondering if she would ever see Shawn again. It had been so much nicer when they were still friends. Then she hadn't worried about whether or not he would call. Everything had automatically changed when Shawn declared homecoming a date. Now the dating rules were back in effect, and Kelsey was remembering too late that she didn't know the rules that applied to Shawn.

"Here's your dinner," the waitress said cheerfully. Kelsey moved her now-empty potato plate to make room for the fish.

"I owe you something," she said, making a halfhearted effort to keep the mood light, even if she felt as if the sky had fallen in on her. She cut her potato, set it on Shawn's small plate, and tried to hand it back to him.

His hand touched the plate, and she assumed he had a good hold on it. But the plate slipped when she let go, and when she tried to grab onto the edge of it, she hit his water glass instead. Horrified, she watched the glass tip and the water seep into the tablecloth and drip off his side of the table.

"I give up," she exclaimed, clasping her hands in her lap before she could cause any more trouble.

"It's all right," he said.

"Sure," she said doubtfully. "Water's dripping on your rented tux, and you tell me everything's all right."

"The water ran off to the side. It missed me." Shawn pushed back his chair to prove his point and bumped into the man at the next table. He excused himself with an embarrassed grin and eased his chair back to its proper spot. "I think we'll be safer if we just eat."

They finished the meal without saying much more. The silence worried Kelsey. She wanted to know what he was thinking. Dating Shawn was the worst thing that had ever happened to her. With other guys, she hadn't really cared when things had gone wrong. She might have been uncomfortable or bored with them, but she had never wanted to crawl off the face of the Earth. For some reason, what Shawn thought of her mattered to Kelsey. And nothing was going to convince her that he wasn't sorry now that he had ever met her. In fact, if he had it to do over again, he probably would find another topic for his history paper. It was all Kelsey could do to keep from bursting into tears.

After he paid the bill, Shawn helped her into her coat and then walked her into the parking lot with an arm wrapped around her. He didn't *seem* angry, but Kelsey didn't want to get her hopes up too high.

"I'll say one thing about you, Kelsey." He looked down at her, with the familiar sparkle in his eyes. "Life isn't boring with you around."

"I guess it's not," she said sadly. She had never intended to become the evening's entertainment.

"Don't sound so glum. I had a good time."

She had to laugh, but it wasn't a happy sound. "Shawn, I warned you that I'm a failure at dating. Why did you fool me? Why did you have to try to prove I was wrong?"

He stopped and placed a hand on each of her shoulders, so he could turn her to face him. Bending his knees so he could look directly into her face, he said, "Let's get one thing straight. I didn't set out to trick you. When I asked you if we could go to homecoming as friends, I was serious. But when I was with you tonight, I realized I didn't feel as if you were just a friend. It was something more."

She licked her lips, touched by his words. "I'm sorry."

He released her and straightened up, running a hand through his hair. "Sorry for what?"

"For letting you think we could date."

"What's there to think about?" He was losing his patience. "We're not thinking about dating. We *are* on a date. And it's not a disaster, unless you turn it into one yourself. I've had a good time."

She wanted to believe him, more than she had ever wanted anything in her life—except to get her braces off the year before. Shyly, she reached a hand out and touched his arm. "Really?"

His arms slipped around her back. "Really," he whispered, leaning over her.

Her breath caught in her throat when she realized what was going to happen. Shawn Horton was going to kiss her! She didn't dare close her eyes. If she didn't watch, she might not believe it had really happened.

His lips were gentle as they touched her mouth. It was a short kiss, but it made her tingle down to her toes. He moved away slowly, with a silly grin on his face.

"I promise, Kelsey, I have never done that before with someone who was just a friend."

Chapter Seven

"So, have you seen Shawn?" Patty asked across the lunch table. Cheryl and Barb leaned closer to hear Kelsey's answer.

"I saw him around school a couple of times yesterday." She tried to sound cheerful, but she didn't feel that way.

He had been so understanding after their disastrous homecoming dinner that she had gone home and dreamed about him. She hadn't planned for things to turn out that way. Shawn had been a good friend, and now she couldn't tell what he felt about her. In fact, she didn't know what she wanted from him. Did she expect him to fuss over her the way guys did around Patty? Or did she want to return to their comfortable friendship?

"Is that all? You've just seen him around school?" Cheryl sounded disappointed.

"You know that everyone's been talking about you and Shawn since homecoming." There was an irritated edge to Patty's voice. "You've got a good thing going—don't blow it."

"It's not up to me," Kelsey complained.

"Sure it is. I saw the way he looked at you Saturday night," Patty argued. "You've got him, if you play it right."

Kelsey wished things were as simple as Patty made them seem. Although she wasn't sure whether she wanted Shawn back as a friend or as more than that, she knew she wanted to see him again. But after she had gotten hives and spilled his water, she didn't feel that it was up to her. Shawn had to decide whether he wanted to risk another date with her.

"Is there room for me?"

The question came from above Kelsey's head, but she recognized the voice, and it made her heart jump. She scooted to the left, making space on the bench. She had to clear her throat to find her voice. "Sit here, Shawn."

Barb shifted to her right to make a little more room for him, and for once, she really did look as if she might faint. Shawn didn't notice, however. His eyes were on Kelsey.

He squeezed ketchup on his chicken sandwich, and Kelsey grimaced. "Do you always put ketchup on chicken?" she asked with her nose still wrinkled.

"Only when it's Spring Hill High chicken." She smiled, and he returned it. "How have you been?"

"Fine." That wasn't true, and she studied her empty plate, so that he wouldn't see the disappointment in her eyes.

"I meant to call you Sunday," he told her as if he had read her mind. "I've been so busy modeling for holiday ads and stuff that I never even see my family. My mother threw my brother and me in the car and made us visit all the grandparents."

"That's okay," she assured him, giggling at the idea of Mrs. Horton *throwing* Shawn into the car. It must have been a sight worth seeing.

Patty clucked her tongue, warning Kelsey that she shouldn't be letting Shawn off so easily. Her friend made sure her guys checked in with her every day, but Kelsey wasn't Patty. And Shawn definitely wasn't a guy who would fall for Patty's games.

"How's chemistry?" he asked before starting on his chicken sandwich.

"You could say I'm surviving." She was pleased he remembered she'd been worried about her chemistry class. "Yesterday we were supposed to use the litmus test to see which beaker had acid in it."

"Sounds exciting," he mumbled around a mouthful of chicken.

"Patty and I discovered acid turns blue litmus paper green."

"Uh, that can't be true," he told her gently. "Believe me. I told you I was good at chemistry last year. Acid turns blue litmus paper red."

"That's what Mr. Truman said, too," Patty interjected, batting her dark lashes at Shawn.

Kelsey tried to feel jealous, but she couldn't. Eyelash fluttering was such an automatic move for Patty that she probably didn't even know she was doing it. Of course, it also made Kelsey feel better that Shawn was trying hard not to laugh at her friend.

"Have you gotten your history paper back?" she asked him.

He nodded and finished his chicken. "I got an A on it."

"Good for you!"

"I really appreciate all the help your mom gave me."

Kelsey blushed even though the compliment was for her mom. "I'll tell her."

"Hey, are you busy next Saturday night?" he asked quickly, his eyes never leaving her face.

Kelsey's palms went cold and sweaty. Was he going to ask her out? Just like that, in front of all her friends?

"I'm not busy at all." Patty sent her a dirty look, and Kelsey knew she was supposed to have played it coy, maybe said something about checking her calendar.

"Would you like to go to the university football game? My brother is playing."

It didn't sound as exciting as homecoming, but she wasn't going to complain. It would be a chance to spend time with Shawn. "Yes, I'd really like that."

"Good. My whole family is going. I'll have to get back to you about the time and all." He started to stand. "I hate to eat and run, but I've got to call my agency before lunch break is over."

He reached out a hand to her, and she took it. His fingers tightened around hers, and she smiled up at him. "Then you'd better get going. Will I see you around?"

"You can count on it." He flashed her a grin like the one her friends had drooled over in the advertisement, and Kelsey heard Barb sigh as he walked away.

"A university football game—not bad," Patty said.

"With his family," Cheryl added.

"Yeah." Kelsey didn't think the family was a bonus. It wouldn't be a very cozy date with his mom and dad along. It crossed her mind that he was bringing them for protection. He had said himself that life wasn't boring with her around. Maybe he was worried about what could happen the next time he was with her.

"Meeting his parents on a second date," Cheryl teased. "It sounds heavy to me."

Patty was smiling so hard her teeth were nearly blinding the people on Kelsey's side of the table. "I am so proud of you!"

The Metrodome was a busy place during the University of Minnesota Gophers game. Kelsey was wedged between Shawn and a stranger; Shawn's parents sat on the other side of him. They were in the second level of seats. She had worried at first that the height might make her nervous, but there was too much to watch to think about how far above the field she was.

Besides the football game, Kelsey was interested in the cheerleading routines and the antics of the person inside the gopher costume. One minute he was jumping with the cheerleaders, and then he would try to capture the other team's mascot.

If that got dull, vendors continually moved up and down the aisles, chanting their wares. "Hot dogs, hot dogs . . ."

"Shawn, are you hungry?"

"Huh?"

"I'm hungry," she said, watching the man with the steaming tray approach. "I'd like a hot dog."

He waved a hand in the air and pulled a rumpled bill from his pocket. His mother took the money and passed it down the row. Seconds later, the hot dog found its way to Kelsey through the same chain of people.

When Kelsey sat back to enjoy the food and watch the game, Shawn leaned forward with his elbows on his knees, as if to study the action carefully. His pose made him look like other Gopher fans in the stands, but there was no hint of concentration on his face. Shawn's eyes weren't focused on the field; they were lost in some kind of dream.

"Boo . . ." Jeers rumbled through the crowd.

Kelsey tugged on Shawn's shirt sleeve. "What happened?"

He turned to her, with a blank look on his face.

"They called off-sides against us, but it looked to me like one of their guys moved first," his mother explained.

Kelsey had missed that while she wondered what was going on with Shawn. He certainly wasn't himself. If he was sick or something, he should have called off the date. She would have understood—maybe.

"All right!" Even Kelsey jumped to her feet when Shawn's brother intercepted a pass from the other team's quarterback.

"Do it, Lee!" Shawn shouted, standing beside her.

She took his hand and squeezed it harder and harder as Lee approached the goal line. The place went crazy when he made the touchdown. Shawn's parents were grinning so hard that she thought they might explode from pride. Kelsey was clapping and screaming like the guy next to her.

When the crowd sat down, the touchdown was replayed on the large video screen, and the crowd cheered again. Then the camera found Lee Horton on the sidelines being congratulated by his teammates. Kelsey caught her breath when she saw the close shot of him. For a second she thought it was Shawn on the screen, and she had to check the seat next to her make sure he was still sitting there.

"Shawn! Are you all right?" Kelsey was shocked. Shawn was slumped back in his seat, his mouth set in a tight, unhappy line. Maybe he knew she'd confused him for a second with his brother. Maybe he was jealous. No, that didn't make sense.

Mrs. Horton leaned over to him and said softly, "You said you wanted to come tonight. You know you didn't have to."

"I know," he mumbled.

Kelsey didn't understand what was going on. Her string of unlucky dates seemed unbroken. Shawn had been so special as a friend, but that night he wasn't the easy-going guy she had come to like. She should have known dating would spoil everything.

"Are you hungry?" he asked after they dropped his parents off at their house.

"No."

Kelsey shivered and pulled her jacket around her. It was a cold night. Shawn's behavior had remained strange throughout the game, and it had played havoc with her nerves. Instead of biting her nails to cope with her worry, she had eaten. After the hot dog she had devoured peanuts, potato chips, ice cream, and a large soda. The last thing she wanted to do now was eat.

"But, Kelsey, we need to talk. Let's go to the Hamburger Hut for something to drink."

"OK." If Shawn wanted to explain his mood, she was willing to suffer a little indigestion. Anyway, she wouldn't sleep that night if she didn't find out why he'd been acting so weirdly.

He slid into the booth beside her, and Kelsey figured that was a good sign. If he had been mad at her for some reason, he would have taken the opposite seat, so he could glare at her.

With an unhappy sigh, he planted his left elbow on the table and rested his chin in his hand. His hair was falling over his forehead, and he closed his eyes before speaking. "I'm sorry about tonight. I was in a terrible mood."

"I figured you were tired or something. Did you work hard this afternoon?" He never talked about his modeling jobs, so she had no idea how exhausting it might be.

"We did a holiday fashion show at the Hartsville mall."

"Why didn't you tell me? I would have come!" She got tingles just thinking about watching Shawn in a show.

"It wasn't important," he said as the waitress arrived. He ordered a soda for each of them.

Wait a minute, Kelsey thought suddenly. *Hartsville?* That's where he had gone to school the last year. Maybe he had seen some old friends, or more specifically, an old girlfriend. She curled her toes in an agony of uncertainty.

"People in Hartsville remember me as a football player," he began slowly. "I saw some old teammates. It reminded me how much I miss playing the game—"

"But you've got something new now. Isn't modeling fun?"

His mouth opened, as if in surprise. "I don't do it for the fun, Kelsey, I do it for the money."

"The money?" Kelsey had assumed that Shawn modeled just because he was gorgeous, glamorous by nature.

The two sodas arrived, and Shawn took a long drink before continuing his explanation. "I want to go to college next fall. My parents expected me to get a football scholarship like my brother, but that's not going to happen now. I'm modeling to earn money for school—if my grades are good enough to get me in."

"You're not dumb, Shawn," she said with conviction.

"I know I'm smart enough to learn to be an

architect, but my high school grades aren't the greatest. I was too busy playing football to study very hard." Shawn shrugged, discouraged. He didn't meet Kelsey's eyes.

"And now you're working so many hours that you still can't get your grades up." It didn't make much sense to Kelsey. He was working so hard to make money for college, that he didn't have time to study. It sounded like he was defeating his own purpose.

She concentrated on her glass for the next few minutes. Worrying about college was pretty heavy, but Shawn couldn't have been thinking about that during the football game. There had to have been something else on his mind.

"Were you feeling sad tonight because your Hartsville friends made you miss the old days?" she asked sympathetically, certain she had it all figured out.

"And watching my brother made me face the fact that I'll never have the future I wanted."

"I don't understand." It made sense that his old Hartsville teammates had given him the business about abandoning football for a modeling career. She knew how insensitive guys could be. But she didn't see where his brother fit in.

Shawn took a deep breath and clenched his hands on the table. His knuckles turned white with the pressure. "*I* was supposed to be on that team with my brother next year. It'll never happen."

"That's a tough break," she told him, hoping she was saying the right thing. Kelsey had no idea what he wanted her to say, or how he wanted her to react. She had never been on a date like this one. Dates were supposed to be fun, but Shawn was telling her his secrets, and she didn't know what to do with them.

"Yeah, it's a real tough break." He drained the last drops from his glass. "Let's go."

Shawn walked to the car slowly, like a man with the weight of the world on his back. He looked so sad that Kelsey could barely stand it. She wondered if Patty would ignore his bad mood and pretend she was having a good time— leaving him to suffer alone—or if she'd try to cheer him up. Or, a better question, would Patty have any idea how to handle this situation at all?

He unlocked her door and opened it. She started to get it, but he took her arm to stop her. "Have I ruined your night? What do you think about all this?"

Standing between him and the car, she struggled for something to say. His hand tightened on her arm, and she knew he was waiting for an answer. She tried to read his eyes in the dark, but she couldn't. Finally the words came from her heart. "I'm not sure what to tell you, except that I'm really sorry things haven't worked out for you."

Before she knew it, she found herself raising

up on her toes to press a gentle kiss against his lips. His arms moved around her, and he hugged her so tightly that she couldn't catch her breath. "Thanks, Kelsey. I needed to hear that, and I need you."

She blinked, astonished. No guy had ever needed her.

Now what was she supposed to do?

Chapter Eight

"Why did you want to meet me so early?" Kelsey asked Shawn, striding across the theater lobby to meet him. "The movie won't start for at least half an hour."

She dropped her car keys into her purse and then took off her glasses to wipe them on the bottom of her powder-blue sweater. He had invited her to the movie on such short notice that she hadn't had time to even clean her glasses, once she discovered Tommy was holding her contacts for ransom.

Shawn stuffed his hands in his pockets and fell into step beside her. "I got some news today that I wanted to talk about," he explained, sounding almost as mysterious as he had on the phone.

He bought their tickets, and they started

toward the auditorium entrance. Shawn paused at the concession stand and asked, "Want some popcorn?"

"No, thanks. My stomach still hasn't recovered from all the junk I ate last night at the football game!"

He led the way and chose seats near the back. Kelsey raised her delicate eyebrows. Either they were going to do a lot of talking or Shawn had some romantic ideas. From the preoccupied look on his face, though, she didn't think he had invited her there to hold hands and whisper sweet nothings into her ear.

"What's with the glasses?" he asked.

Just what she needed—small talk. She had been starting her English assignment when he called. Instead of staying home to read the first half of *The Scarlet Letter*, she had rushed out to meet Shawn. He had made it sound so important, and now he wanted to talk about her glasses!

"Tommy kidnapped my contact lenses and is holding them for ransom. What do you think about that?"

"I think I'm lucky I don't have a little brother." He tried to smile, but only one side of his mouth curved. "The modeling agency called me today," he said casually.

"On Sunday?"

"It's the end of October. This is a pressure time for retailers planning their Christmas attacks. They have me scheduled for two department store catalogs and a lot of other things."

"That's fantastic!" Kelsey didn't understand why he was acting so glum about it. "If you need money for college, this must be good news."

"But I've got a ton of homework through the end of the quarter. I'm not very good at writing term papers, and I've got three of them to do."

Maybe he wants help with them, Kelsey thought. Although, if he'd ever seen the way she went about researching and writing papers, he wouldn't be asking for her assistance. He must have something else in mind. "Is there something I can do?"

"There sure is." He reached over the armrest to take her hand. "It would help a lot if you could be understanding."

Although she knew what it was like to have lots of homework, she didn't know about trying to juggle a job, too. Her parents only scheduled her at the health club over vacations and during emergencies. "I can try to understand," she said, making her best offer.

"I think you missed the point, Kelsey. If I'm going to be modeling after school every day and all day on the weekends, I'll have to use what free time is left to study. I have to pull decent grades this quarter, so I can apply to the university."

If he was going to be working and studying evenings and during the weekends, he wasn't going to have time for her. Kelsey almost choked before voicing the one question she hoped she'd never need to ask Shawn. "Are you saying you don't want to see me anymore?"

"I'm saying I won't *be able* to see you for a few weeks," he said in a tired voice.

Kelsey wondered if he was already exhausted from working and studying, or if he was bored with her. Last night, when they had kissed, he seemed to like her, but now she had an uneasy feeling.

When she didn't speak, he cleared his throat. "It's the best I can do. I can't turn down the jobs, and I can't afford to fail my classes."

"I know you can't," she said, trying to sound sympathetic. Shawn was making her feel selfish for wanting to see him. Of course she didn't want him to get bad grades, and she wouldn't expect him to stop working. But really! Was it too much to ask to see him once in a while? He could at least have lunch with her at school or call her during breaks on his modeling shoots.

He squeezed her hand. "I really appreciate your patience, Kelsey. I didn't know if you would be this understanding about my being booked through the first weekend of December."

"December!" she exclaimed. She had thought he was talking about not seeing her for a week or two. Over a month was a long time. Long enough for feelings to change, hers and Shawn's both.

Kelsey had heard enough good-byes to recognize what Shawn was really telling her. He didn't expect her to be waiting for him in December.

The lights lowered, and the coming attractions appeared on the screen. She slumped down in her seat and pulled her hand free from his. He rested his head against the back of the chair, with his arms folded across his chest. He didn't seem to mind in the least that she had returned his hand.

By the time the movie started, she noticed Shawn's breathing had become slow and regular. She nudged his arm, and nothing happened. This topped everything that had happened on the other dates. He had fallen asleep!

She wasn't sure if it was common sense or Patty's dating rules that insisted that Shawn could find time for her in his busy schedule. It was clear that he was dumping her. But things had started out so well for them. Where had she gone wrong?

On their first date she had gotten hives, but he had acted as if it didn't matter. It was true, he had a smooth style, but even suave Shawn couldn't have covered up his disgust, if that had really bothered him.

Their second date had been the game the night before, and she still couldn't explain exactly what had gone wrong there. He had been in a bad mood, and he had said he needed her.

It must have been some sort of test. Most likely she had failed.

And their third date, if she could call this movie affair a date . . .

Wait a minute! Kelsey's brain screamed. This was their *third* date, and she had never managed to have a fourth date with any guy. She should have seen it coming! Covering her face with her hands, she wished with all her heart that she had told Shawn she was too busy to meet him at the movies that afternoon.

Shawn had been special. They had been so comfortable together when they were just friends. It was that easy feeling that had encouraged her to trust again, and after all her disastrous dates, she had been stupid enough to hope things would be different with Shawn. How many times would she have to be hurt before she learned—really learned—that Kelsey Kramer was better off without dates? Boys were nothing except trouble.

When she realized she didn't care about the movie, and that she didn't want to see Shawn when he woke up, Kelsey dug for her car keys in her purse and walked out of the theater. She could have stayed there and cried in the dark, but she thought she'd rather do that at home in her own room.

"Kelsey, it's a *party*. Cheer up."

She looked up at her mother from a chair in

the corner of Jill's apartment. "I don't feel very happy."

"I know you're upset about Shawn, but you could stop being so stubborn. Since you left him at the movie, I think it's up to you to apologize."

"You don't understand," Kelsey argued. Mrs. Kramer shrugged, then patted Kelsey's cheek and went back to her spot on the sofa.

Friends and family had decided to throw a surprise bridal shower for Jill in her own apartment. And Jill had been very surprised when she came home from work! Everyone had spilled out of her bedroom, shouting congratulations and piling gifts up on the coffee table. Only Kelsey had stayed in the bedroom for an extra five minutes. She just didn't feel festive.

She was exhausted from avoiding Shawn at school. In the past she had been able to face her ex-dates. It was different with Shawn. Of course, it was her own fault for letting herself care about him as a boyfriend, but she had never hurt this badly before. She just couldn't handle running into him at school.

Bits of passing conversations caught Kelsey's attention as people started to carry their paper plates out to the kitchen. Apparently it was time for Jill to open her presents. Kelsey took her trash into the other room. When she returned, her chair had been moved into the center of the room, where a circle was being made around the coffee table. She sat with two of Jill's friends so she wouldn't have to talk to her mom about Shawn any more.

"Just six weeks until the wedding. How can you stand it?" someone asked as Jill opened a blender.

How am I going to stand it? Kelsey asked herself. Six weeks of people talking about love and weddings. Before, she had sort of been joking when she acted as though the wedding bothered her, but now it really did. Love worked for Jill and for Patty. Why did Kelsey always have to be the loser?

"Where are you going for the honeymoon?"

"Hawaii." Everyone groaned, jealous that Jill would be escaping Minnesota in December. She simply smiled. "Eric picked up the tickets today."

"Will you be moving into Eric's apartment or yours?" Kelsey's neighbor asked.

"Neither. My lease is up at the end of the year, and who would want to move into Eric's place?" Jill made a face, and Kelsey's mom laughed the hardest. They always joked that the things growing in Eric's refrigerator could probably cure half the diseases in the world.

Jill opened another box and pulled out a set of peach bath towels. "The color is just perfect!"

"Have you found a place yet?" Sue, one of Jill's bridesmaids, asked.

"We've signed the lease on a duplex near my office. It'll almost be like having a house." Kelsey had never heard Jill sound so dreamy. She was really getting carried away with the domestic stuff.

"Have fun moving. It's a lot of work," the woman on Kelsey's other side said.

"That's right! You just moved into a new house. How is it?" Jill talked without looking up, since she was tugging on a knotted ribbon.

"It's OK. I'll like it better when I find my youngest son. We figure he's in one of the cartons in the basement. Seriously, I'll save my boxes for you."

"That would be great."

It was just too cute, Kelsey decided. While she was facing life alone, everyone here seemed to have boyfriends, husbands, and kids. She was so bored, she decided, she'd rather be home finishing *The Scarlet Letter*.

Two girls started giggling when Jill finally got the box open and blushed a deep red. Slowly she lifted a flimsy pink nightgown out of the wrapping.

Everyone hooted. Everyone except Kelsey. All this love and stuff was too much for her. Faking a cough that wouldn't stop, she excused herself and got a glass of water in the kitchen. She stayed out there for a few minutes and tried to improve her attitude. It was a party, after all, and even her mom was having fun. Why shouldn't she have a good time, too?

"It's time for *Mason Carter*," someone exclaimed in the living room, naming a popular detective series. "That's my favorite show."

"Mine, too. What a hunk! Jill, do you mind if we turn it on?"

Jill laughed. "Go ahead."

Kelsey stood in the kitchen doorway and watched. They had turned on the TV just as the program was fading into a commercial.

"Darn! Hey, wait. He's not bad," one of the Mason Carter fans commented.

Kelsey snorted in disgust. It sounded like these women drooled over men as easily as Patty and her other friends. She didn't bother to check out the guy on the screen.

"Isn't that Sh—" Jill's voice was suddenly cut off, and Kelsey peeked into the room to find her mother's hand over Jill's mouth.

"Do you know him?" Sue asked.

"I thought he looked like Kelsey's— Ouch!" Jill cringed as Mrs. Kramer kicked her in the ankle. "Kelsey's a big girl. Why are you protecting her?"

"Protecting me from what?" Kelsey stepped into the living room.

"Look." Jill pointed to the television.

"Shawn!"

She knew he'd been working a lot, but he never mentioned doing a television commercial for a local restaurant. Her knees went weak, and she had to sit in the nearest chair. Staring at the screen, where Shawn was sharing his dessert with a gorgeous brunette, Kelsey barely heard the voices around her.

"So, who is he?"

"Her boyfriend."

"Her ex-boyfriend."

"He's in high school?"

"Yeah. Can you believe it?"

"Is this the guy, the one who was just a friend, that you were talking about at the dress fittings?" Sue asked.

It seemed like ages since they had met at the bridal salon for their fittings. Kelsey remembered Jill telling her to invite a boy to the wedding and teasing her about Shawn. So much had happened since then. Unwelcome tears came to Kelsey's eyes when she remembered talking with Shawn about guys while they did the jigsaw puzzle. And he had been so understanding about the hives and all. Would she ever know what had gone wrong?

"Hey, Kelsey." Jill's voice was gentle when she knelt next to the chair. "I didn't mean to upset you. But you can't hibernate for the winter just because Shawn has hurt you."

"But, Jill . . ." Kelsey's throat choked up. Her lips were quivering too much for her to speak.

"You don't have to explain anything right now. If you want to talk about it sometime, give me a call."

Jill sounded as if she wanted to say more, but her friends were calling her back. Kelsey really didn't want to spoil the party, so she wiped away the one tear that was ready to fall down her cheek and tried to smile. She pretended to be watching Jill, but her mind was busy.

She wasn't going to let Shawn Horton ruin her life. Kelsey Kramer had survived Rick the Rat and Jon the Joker; she would make it through Shawn, too. And someday she might understand why Shawn had gotten tired of her so quickly.

Chapter Nine

"Kelsey Kramer!"

The voice was rough, but she recognized it along with the touch on her arm. For over a week she had brought her lunch from home and eaten it in the halls in order to avoid him. She had been late for chemistry five days in a row because she took the long way around the school, so she wouldn't cross his path.

After a long talk she and Patty had figured out that Shawn had just wanted to prove he could get the nondater to date. Knowing that, Kelsey had spared no energy to keep out of his way.

"What do you want, Shawn?" She kept her voice calm and disinterested.

He was going up the stairs, and she was two steps below him heading in the other direction.

She didn't like bending her neck back to look at him, especially when she saw the expression on his face. His lips were tight, and his eyes seemed to be looking right through her.

"I want to know what's going on," he told her. "You seem to have disappeared off the face of the earth, starting with your little trick at the theater a week ago Sunday. And your friends all turn their backs when I see them in the hall."

A laughing couple was coming down the stairs, and Shawn stepped behind her to let them pass. His books were tucked under one arm, while his other arm rested on the railing. When she didn't respond, even after the couple had disappeared, he jammed the free hand into his jacket pocket. "I can understand your being disappointed that I'm too busy to see much of you for a few weeks, but aren't you carrying it a little too far?"

"Me? *I'm* carrying it a little too far?" Kelsey's arms fell limp at her sides, and her purse slid off her shoulder. His accusations were unreal. Did he expect her to smile and wave at him in the halls as if nothing had happened? No boy who had dumped her had ever complained about her not being friendly afterward.

He breathed a deep sigh, tipping his head back to study the ceiling. "What's going on here? You're treating me like I've got the plague or something." Rubbing the back of his neck, he looked down at her. "Kelsey, if you don't want to see me anymore, be straight enough to tell me."

If she didn't want to see *him* anymore? She would have hocked the family TV if it would have meant getting Shawn Horton back. Or at least, *before* she and Patty had figured out his game, she would have done that.

"And what do you know about being straight with someone?" she challenged, walking down the stairs to the hall floor. "It must have made you feel good, being the new kid in school and all."

"What are you talking about?" he asked, joining her.

She gave him credit for looking truly bewildered. It was probably some technique he had learned modeling. "Was your ego satisfied when *you* were the one guy who could make me change my mind about dating? Did it make you feel important?"

He touched his hands to his forehead like a person with a throbbing headache. "Let me get this right. You think I pursued you and wore down your defenses just so I could say I'd dated the undatable Kelsey Kramer?"

"Something like that," she answered. His sarcastic tone made it sound like a stupid theory. But Kelsey knew the truth when she heard it; she wasn't going to let him fool her again.

"Could I ask when you came up with this story? Or should I ask if you had help with it?"

"Patty and I were talking about—"

He rolled his eyes, and that angered Kelsey. "Don't do that! Patty knows a lot about guys. Anyway, after you dumped me, she realized that you'd been trying to prove you were a *real man* by changing my mind about dating. And once you had done that, there was nothing left between us."

He stretched to his full height and stared down at her, his eyes clearly telling her he wasn't buying the story. His voice was surprisingly mild when he asked, "Do you really believe I'd do that to you?"

"Well, sure."

"Even if I promise you homecoming was the best date I've ever had?" he asked her.

The best date? He had to be kidding! But if she thought he was lying, why was something fluttering in her stomach? "Maybe Patty went a little too far with her theory," Kelsey grudgingly admitted.

"Just a little too far? I'm the guy who ate dinner with your whole family, including Tommy, just so I could see you again after that first night. Remember?"

She swallowed hard, fighting back her desire to believe him. "If you liked me so much, why did you dump me at the theater—"

"I dumped *you* at the movies?" Shawn laughed

grimly and shook his head. "I thought I was the one who woke up alone and abandoned."

"Sure, I left you there after you'd told me to take a hike. Of course, you said it in much nicer terms." He opened his mouth, but Kelsey wouldn't let him interrupt. "I shouldn't have been surprised. After all, you were just fitting into my usual dating pattern."

"Am I supposed to know what that means?" He shoved his left hand back into his pocket.

"It's simple." He wasn't going to intimidate her. "No guy has ever asked me out more than three times. There's no reason you should be any different."

Shawn sort of sagged. He reminded Kelsey of a balloon after someone had let the air out. She should have been relieved when the anger seeped out of his body, but the look in his eyes cut right to her heart. He looked so hurt.

"I don't believe you." His voice was scratchy, the way Kelsey's sounded when she was all choked up. "I thought there was something special between us. You know, the kind of relationship where you would tell me if you thought anything was going wrong. If you'd cared about me at all, you wouldn't have given up so easily—"

"Of course I cared about you," she argued. "I wouldn't be hurting this much if I hadn't cared—"

"Don't interrupt." His sharp command silenced

her. "I should have listened to the guys when they tried to warn me about you."

"What did they say?" There was a sinking feeling in Kelsey's stomach. It was possible she might not want to know what the boys said about her.

"They thought you had some pretty weird ideas about dating even before you gave it up. I told myself it was just talk, but this giving a guy just three chances to be perfect is ridiculous."

"It's never been up to me! No one ever wants to see me more than three times."

"I did," he said softly. "I wish you had told me about your rules. I would have behaved better so you wouldn't have needed to throw me away."

"I don't understand . . ." Kelsey's head was spinning.

"I bet you don't." Shawn started up the steps. "Why don't you think about it? You might learn something."

After his footsteps faded away, Kelsey leaned against the wall, thinking. What was going on? Patty's conclusions had seemed extremely logical. And her own explanation that the three-date phenomenon had taken over Shawn had made sense. There was just one problem: He didn't seem to think he had ever dumped her.

That was crazy! A girl knew when a boy told her to get lost. Didn't she?

*   *   *

"We've got to talk." Kelsey charged breathlessly into Patty's house and led the way to their family room. Dropping onto the couch, she peeled off her jacket as she sat. It hadn't made sense to go home first when she needed so much help. Patty was the one with all the answers.

"Will you tell me what's wrong?" Patty ran down the steps behind Kelsey and sat at the other end of the couch, looking concerned. "You're paler than a ghost."

"Don't be cute. This is serious. I just saw Shawn."

"Oh." Patty put a world into that single syllable. She turned toward Kelsey and tucked her legs beneath her. "Tell me what happened."

If she knew exactly what had happened, she wouldn't have been sitting on Patty's couch falling to pieces. With all her jumbled thoughts racing through her mind, it was hard to decide where to start. The beginning seemed like the best place. "I ran into him in the stairway after school. Was he ever mad at me!"

Patty's mouth fell open. "He was mad at *you*? Why? *He's* the one who decided things were over between the two of you."

"That was exactly how I felt!" Kelsey pushed up the sleeves of her Icelandic sweater just to have something to do with her nervous hands. Then she tugged them back down.

"Men!" Patty snorted. "I bet he even tried to

132

convince you he hadn't taken you out just to prove to the guys that Kelsey Kramer could be persuaded to date."

"Actually, something more amazing happened. He didn't seem to know it was all over between us." She hoped she had that right. It had been a confusing conversation, but he had acted, at least at first, as if they were a *couple* having a fight.

"Wait a minute." Patty paused impressively. "You told me he broke up with you at the movies. Either he did or he didn't. What's the deal?"

"I thought he did."

"What does that mean?" Patty squinted her eyes and seemed determined to uncover all the facts.

"Well, what was I supposed to think when he started telling me how busy he was going to be and that he wouldn't have time for me?"

"I see your point." Patty nodded thoughtfully. "From my experience, those are definite exit lines."

"But are you sure that's what Shawn meant?" Kelsey worried aloud. "I mean, you're the one who said Shawn Horton didn't play by your rules."

Patty glared. She hated having her authority challenged. "Look, if you don't think I can help you, then why did you come over here to talk?"

"I'm sorry," Kelsey promised. "I'm just so confused. What if Shawn really did still like me, until today? I might have blown the best thing that ever happened to me!"

"Sometimes that just happens." Patty picked at a snag in the couch cushion. "My life isn't so perfect right now, either."

"Things aren't going well with Cliff, the football hero?" Kelsey was stunned. Except for T.J., Patty never had problems with guys. They always did what she wanted them to do.

"No. Things are pretty bad, and I don't know what to do." Patty's voice was soft and concerned.

Kelsey would never have dreamed that Patty could run out of strategies. "Did you have a fight?"

"Not exactly." Patty's hand pressed against her cheek as she heaved a dramatic sigh. "Last night he told me I'm no different from all the other girls who flirt with him."

Kelsey's eyes widened. How could any guy say her best friend was just like all the other girls? "What does he want from you?"

"How should I know? He says he needs a girl who is special, but I have no idea what I need to do to be that girl."

"Can you ask him?" Patty frowned, and Kelsey realized she was sounding like Jill. "I mean, has he given you any hints?"

"All he ever talks about are the scouts watching his football games. Every time people from college football staffs are in town, he's a wreck from the pressure."

"That would be hard." She couldn't help thinking of Shawn. He would much rather have the pressure of playing with scouts in the stands than not be playing at all.

"Sure, it's hard." Patty waved her hand as if to say her boyfriend's concerns weren't the biggest problem here. "But he's ruining *my* life. What does he expect from me? What am I supposed to do?"

"I don't know. And I don't know what I'm supposed to do about Shawn. He's probably going to hate me forever."

"Hate you forever? Aren't you exaggerating?" Patty asked indifferently. "If he said good-bye, then he's done with you. He'll be too busy with someone else to spend his time hating you."

Patty's sympathy had seemed to evaporate when she mentioned her own problem. Kelsey didn't appreciate the way her friend was trying to make Shawn sound like a lost cause just so they could talk about Cliff some more. "For your information, Shawn didn't tell me good-bye."

"So what did he say?" Patty asked.

"Something about my learning what I had done wrong. . . ." That was the most sense Kelsey could make of his parting comments.

"Do you have any ideas?" Interest sparked in Patty's voice.

"Sorry, Patty. I don't have a clue."

And she was sorry because it crossed her mind they could be having the same kind of problems with their guys. If she and Patty could figure out what just one of the guys wanted, it might help them solve the puzzle of the other. Too bad neither one of them had any answers.

Kelsey skipped dinner to lie down and think. She hadn't stayed at Patty's house very long. Their discussion had depressed Patty so much that Kelsey figured she had a better chance of cheering herself up on her own.

The one thing that she couldn't get out of her mind was the hurt look on Shawn's face. He had clearly been disappointed in her, but it was beyond Kelsey's ability to see how she had failed him. She had agreed to date him when he thought it was a good idea. And she had tried to be a sport when he was having a hard time. There didn't seem to be a lot more she could have done.

Talking to Patty had shown Kelsey one thing. They had believed they could get boyfriends by smiling at them and saying the right things. But that wasn't good enough for Patty's boyfriend, and apparently it hadn't been enough for Shawn either. Both of those guys could take their pick of dozens of girls who acted just right, but they wanted someone special.

She remembered what Shawn had whispered to her that night after the football game. *I need you.* It had scared her at the time, and she still didn't know what he meant by it. What had he needed her for? He had asked for understanding, but she had never understood just what it was he wanted her to understand.

All the ideas galloping in her brain made her head hurt. She rested on the pillow and threw an arm over her eyes. It was funny to remember how she had felt with Rick the Rat. She had assumed that would be the biggest mess in her whole life.

Back then, she had had no idea how bad things could really get. It occurred to Kelsey that maybe none of this had anything to do with her. Maybe boys were just getting stranger. Considering Patty's problem, that seemed like a logical explanation. If the time had come for a guy to be unhappy with Patty, then the world had gone crazy.

On the other hand, maybe life just got harder as people got older. She thought of Jill. Kelsey's efforts to get ready for homecoming had been nothing compared to the work it was taking to put together a wedding. And while she worried about having a date for the weekend, Jill was going to have to find a way to live with her brother forever.

She sat up in bed. That was it! Quickly she dialed the phone. "Jill?"

"Is that you, Kelsey?"

"Yes. Remember you said we could talk sometime?" She crossed her fingers that Jill would have time for her right away.

"Sure. When would you like to get together?"

"Tonight." Kelsey held her breath.

"I'll meet you at the Hamburger Hut in half an hour."

Finally something was going right! Jill knew about friends, love, and men. She was guaranteed to have the answers.

Chapter Ten

"What's the emergency?" Jill asked, sliding into the seat across from Kelsey.

"I saw Shawn today." Kelsey pushed a sandy-blond strand out of her eyes.

"Was it the first time you've seen him since he ended things with you?" Jill's voice was full of sympathy.

"Yeah. I'd been doing a pretty good job of avoiding him, but my luck ran out." Although she knew the Hamburger Hut's menu by heart, Kelsey pretended to look it over. Her emotions were so overworked that she thought she might break down even just talking about Shawn one more time.

"Was it difficult?"

She nodded her answer, as the waitress approached. Jill ordered apple pie à la mode, but

Kelsey just asked for a soda. She had come there to talk, not to eat.

"Are you going to tell me what happened?" Jill asked finally when Kelsey remained quiet.

"I found out he hadn't asked me out just because I was a challenge—"

"A challenge?"

"You remember when I told you how I thought he'd dated me just so he could say he had taken out the girl who had given up guys?" They had discussed Shawn briefly after dinner at the house last weekend.

"Sure, I remember," Jill said, sounding as if the concept hadn't impressed her. "I never thought you were serious about it. Shawn seemed like a nice guy to me. He wouldn't have done something so mean."

"He pointed that out this afternoon," Kelsey said, wincing now at the thought of how dumb she must have seemed when she accused him of deceiving her.

"Was it painful?" Jill asked softly.

"More like embarrassing, but then I made it worse by telling him it was all right that he had dropped me, that I understood what had happened because no guy has ever dated me more than three times."

"Really? Only three dates?" Jill looked intrigued.

"I know it's weird. I figure it's fate or something." Their order came, and Kelsey took a long sip of her drink and then blew some bubbles into it with her straw.

"I think it's more likely a coincidence." Jill sank her fork into a warm piece of pie swimming in vanilla ice cream. "What did Shawn say when you suggested he had fallen into your regular pattern?"

"He seemed really disappointed that I would think we had broken up over something so stupid."

"Did he ever say why he did call things off?"

Kelsey took a few seconds to stir her soda with the straw. "Oh. Didn't I mention that he didn't think it was over?"

Jill coughed, choking on a bite of pie. "What?"

"I was confused, too, when it happened." *Confused* seemed like a trivial word for what she had felt at the time. "He thought I'd been avoiding him because I was mad at him for being busy. When I said something about him dumping me, he had no idea what I meant."

Jill waved to the waitress and ordered a cup of black coffee. "This is getting interesting," she told Kelsey. "Did you solve all your troubles by telling him you'd made a mistake?"

Kelsey rolled her eyes. "Of course not. Instead of being smart and making up, *that's* when I explained the three-date phenomenon! I feel sick just remembering what he said next. He told me he had thought our relationship was special. He said I should have come to him if I thought something was wrong. And he looked so hurt! I wish we had just stayed friends and never dated!"

Kelsey took a long drink to soothe her dry throat. Across the table, Jill tilted her head and peered at her. Kelsey had teachers who looked at her that way after she gave incredibly stupid answers in class. She didn't see that she had said anything that was so strange.

"Are you convinced that everything went downhill just because you and Shawn started dating?"

"Sure. We had a great time as friends, and then he wanted to turn it into something more. I knew it was a mistake, but how could I turn him down when I liked being with him so much?"

"I guess I don't know about all your disasters with Shawn. I've heard about homecoming and the hives. You made it sound like he was a great date and a sensitive guy."

Kelsey smiled. "He was wonderful that night."

"So when did it go bad?"

"It started when he took me to his brother's football game. He was really down that night. Personally, I don't know why he invited me to the game if it was going to upset him that way. Afterward, he told me how much he missed playing."

"That sounds positive to me."

"Positive?" Kelsey thought Jill must have misunderstood. "The guy was telling me all his secret feelings. I didn't know what to do!"

"You could have listened," Jill suggested.

The memory of Shawn saying he *needed* her popped into Kelsey's mind. Could he have meant he needed her to listen as a friend? The same way she and Patty had started out listening to each other that afternoon?

"You should see your face!" Jill couldn't help but laugh. "You went from biting your lip to squinting thoughtfully to shaking your head. What are you thinking?"

"I was wondering if Shawn could've been telling me his problems the same way I would talk to Patty, or you, about something that bothered me." She stopped to think it over one more time. "If that's true, then I should have listened and tried to help him. But it couldn't be true."

Jill's eyes opened wide. "Why not? Why couldn't Shawn have decided to share something important with you instead of one of his other friends?"

Kelsey licked her lips. She was trying very hard to believe he could have needed her that way, but it still seemed impossible. "He just couldn't have," she said finally. "Shawn's a *guy*."

Jill shook her head in confusion. "Tell me if I'm way off base here, but it sounds like you think men are a whole separate species that was dropped off by an alien space ship. Am I close?"

Kelsey was offended that Jill could joke around

when she had come to her for serious advice. "Of course they're not aliens. I'm just saying guys are different, and I don't understand how they think or how they work."

"But, Kelsey, men have the same kinds o[f] feelings that women have—at least most men do. Not every boy is going to tell you his fears and dreams, but Shawn trusted you enough t[o] share what was in his heart. That should have been like a gift to you."

It hadn't felt like a present that night. Kelsey squirmed as she recollected her confusion. She tried to explain. "But it made me feel so uncom[-] fortable."

"Sharing confidences can be awkward," Jil[l] admitted. "Haven't any of your girlfriends ever come to you with secrets that are hard to keep? Ones that you would rather not know, but you listen, anyway, because you're a friend?"

"Sure." Kelsey could think of lots of exam[-] ples. "Sometimes it would be easier not to know their problems with their parents or their boy friends, but being there for them is part o[f] being a friend."

Jill nodded. "Don't you consider yourself t[o] be one of Shawn's friends?"

"We used to be friends. . . ." Kelsey's voice trailed off, and she stared down at her hands. She had been so sure friendship ended when [d]ating began. It hadn't occurred to her tha[t] [r]eal friends didn't stop being friends so quickly.

"Maybe we're still friends, and I just didn't know it until now."

"Friendship is a good beginning," Jill said, fingering her diamond ring. "Eric and I have been friends a long time, and that makes our love more special, because we know each other so well."

"You think people can still be friends even after things get romantic between them?" It was hard for Kelsey to believe.

"It happened to me." Jill shrugged. "I'm not an expert on love. I only know what's happened in my own experience. What do *you* expect from your friends?"

"When I'm good friends with someone, like Patty, we care about each other, and we trust each other."

"Would you want that same kind of relationship with a guy like Shawn, maybe with a little romance thrown in as a bonus?"

Kelsey closed her eyes as she began to understand Jill's point. "I've cared about Shawn and trusted him since the first night he came to my house. And it's pretty clear now that he felt the same way about me. How did I mess it up so badly?"

Jill smiled. "Considering your experience with insensitive guys and the three-date routine, I'm not surprised you didn't understand that Shawn was reaching out to you as a real friend. He wanted to share his feelings about football and

his worries about his future with you, and you
didn't know how to react."

"That's exactly it. I couldn't think of anything
to say!" If this made sense to Jill, Kelsey thought,
then maybe there was a chance Shawn could
understand it and take her back.

"There was nothing wrong with feeling uncomfortable," Jill told her. "But Shawn was probably hoping for some patience and a friendly
ear."

And she hadn't offered to help him at all. A
painful question nagged at Kelsey's brain, killing the hopes that were trying to surface. "But
do you think he could still care about me, after
I was such a failure when he needed a friend?"

"Didn't you say he was hurt that you believed
he only wanted three dates?"

"He was sorry I had given up on him so easily."

"Doesn't that tell you something?" Jill's face
brightened with the determination to make
Kelsey understand. "When you accepted losing
him, or at least thinking you had lost him, it
made him feel like you didn't care about him. If
he didn't still like you a lot, why would it hurt
him to think you would let him go without a
fight?"

Kelsey had to agree with Jill. If Shawn didn't
still like her, he wouldn't care whether or not
she had a good reason for avoiding him. He
would have just been glad to be rid of her.

"I see what you mean. If I were Shawn, I'd be

insulted that a girl I still cared about hadn't trusted me."

"Congratulations!" Jill clapped her hands and grinned. "If you can start to see Shawn's point of view, then I know you're starting to believe that boys are people who can hurt and worry, just like girls."

"I guess it's time I quit using Patty's rules and began to follow my own instincts." Kelsey smiled, but then her smile faded. She would look for Shawn the next day at school, but she didn't know whether he would talk to her or not. "But, Jill, do you think I have a chance to get him back?"

"Maybe. Shawn is a special person. He deserves a girl who is willing to share the good times and still be there for him when things aren't going so well. Are you willing to do that?"

There wasn't any doubt in Kelsey's mind. "Of course I want to do all that for Shawn. Do you think he's going to let me?"

"That's up to you." Jill made it sound like a challenge.

Suddenly Kelsey's appetite returned. She was up to the challenge, but she couldn't begin figuring out how to win Shawn back on an empty stomach. "I hope you don't have anything else to do right now, Jill. I need a hot-fudge sundae!"

The day after her talk with Jill, Kelsey looked for Shawn in school—with no luck. She was beginning to wonder if he had changed his routine to avoid her because she didn't find him in any of his regular places.

She had gulped down her lunch and told the others she had to study in the library. Actually, though, she had left because she couldn't take much more of Patty. It had seemed like a good idea to tell Patty what she had learned from Jill, but that turned out to be a major mistake.

"Tell guys what you really think? Treat them like friends?" Patty had almost fainted. She had been thrilled that Kelsey was going to try to get Shawn back, but she didn't approve of her strategy.

Kelsey couldn't help giggling at Patty's instructions. Patty told her to find Shawn and then pretend to lose one of her contact lenses. She could say it was still in her eye somewhere, and then Shawn would have to get awfully close to her to help her find it. Or, she could say it had fallen on the floor, and they could crawl around together looking for it.

After Shawn's homecoming compliment—that he liked her because she was natural—Kelsey knew she didn't want to resort to games. He deserved better. She was determined to offer him an honest apology—until she actually saw him in person, talking to another guy outside the library door.

Panic paralyzed her breathing and turned her hands clammy. Maybe this was how boys felt every time they approached a girl for a date. How awful! *Enough is enough,* she told herself sternly. Wanting to be a better friend to Shawn was a good idea, but she didn't have to get carried away with pity for every guy who had ever asked her out.

She fingered the envelope hidden inside her notebook, making sure she could pull it out quickly if all went well. The boy talking to Shawn glanced at her and then nodded in her direction. Slowly Shawn turned around.

This was it. He had seen her. It was too late to chicken out now. Kelsey waited for him to respond in some way, not caring whether he smiled or frowned. All she wanted to know was where she stood with him, but he showed no emotion. He looked like Shawn Horton, the model, his face a handsome, unreadable mask.

It was going to be harder than she expected. Hoping he wouldn't notice, she dipped her head and closed her right eyelid. She blinked twice, desperately trying to dislodge her contact lens. *What am I doing?*

His friend had left, but Shawn was still hesitating at the library door. She hoped he was waiting for her; that would be a good sign. Before she could try any more tricks with her contacts, despite herself, she walked boldly up to him.

"Hi, Shawn." Her voice cracked. How humiliating. That wasn't quite the impression she wanted to make.

"I didn't expect to see you today." His expression still hid emotion. He had a cautious look in his eyes, and his voice was steady.

When she pasted a smile on her face, her lip promptly stuck to her gum. Pretending to yawn, Kelsey covered her mouth and fixed her lips. "Excuse me. I must be tired."

He shifted his weight to one side, but he showed no other signs of impatience until he spoke. "Did you want something, Kelsey? I'm supposed to be researching a paper."

"I'm sorry," she whispered.

"For keeping me out of the library or for something more?"

Kelsey studied his face, waiting for some sign that he would accept a real apology. His face could have been carved in marble. Instead of helping her, he took a step toward the library.

"Wait. I guess I'm sorry for both things." She held her breath, waiting for him to say something, but just then another guy stopped next to Shawn.

"Are you ready for that economics test, Horton?"

"Can fish fly?" he joked, as if he had completely forgotten Kelsey was trying to apologize to him.

"I know what you mean," his friend said. "There's no hope for me, either."

How long was Shawn going to chat about this test? Kelsey tapped her foot anxiously. She wondered if she had ever kept a guy waiting this way, once he had gathered all his courage to approach her. She hoped she had never been that insensitive, and if she had been, she promised herself never to do it again, if only Shawn would forgive her and give her another chance.

Suddenly Shawn was reaching for her. His hand merely touched her elbow, but Kelsey felt like an electric shock had jolted through her body. The other boy had disappeared.

"You were saying you were sorry," Shawn hinted.

There was a shade of hope in his eyes, and that was enough to get Kelsey started. She realized at that moment that she had been nervously biting her fingernail, and she felt her cheeks go pink. "Yes, Shawn. I overreacted when you tried to explain your busy holiday schedule, and I was very unfair not to tell you how I felt—"

"Not to mention that it wasn't very nice of you to leave me at the theater." Now his mouth was trying to turn up at the corners.

She nodded, the confession going easier as she got into it. "Yeah, that was pretty rude."

"I hate to ask this, but are you apologizing just to clear your conscience?"

"What do you mean?"

"I want to know if we're making up. Are you

apologizing because you admit we belong to-gether? Or are you saying you're sorry just so you don't feel like such a rat for dumping me?"

"I didn't dump you," Kelsey exclaimed. "And you don't seem to think you broke up with me. So it *looks* like we're still a team." She sounded more confident than she felt.

"That's all right with me." Shawn smiled at her the way he used to, his green eyes spar-kling, and she melted.

"You mean you're willing to forget all the things I've done?" Kelsey was astonished. If he agreed to that, then she'd know he was too good to be true.

"I won't forget *everything*. . . ."

"I was afraid of that." She sighed. Now they would have to work out a compromise.

"Don't jump to conclusions. Remember how that got you into trouble last time," he said. "I meant that I don't want to forget everything that has happened between us. Too many of the memories are good."

Kelsey knew at that moment that she didn't deserve Shawn, but she was going to keep him anyway. It was time for her big move. Sucking in a deep breath, she pulled the beige envelope out of the top of her notebook. "I have some-thing for you."

He took it from her, and she swore his hands were shaking as he pulled the invitation out of the envelope. After unfolding the heavy paper, he studied it. Kelsey's palms itched from nerves while she waited. The verse in Jill and Eric's wedding invitation wasn't that long. What was he thinking? To quote Barb, she was going to die if he didn't look up soon.

When he lowered the invitation and his eyes met hers, Kelsey knew it had been worth the wait. His eyes were shining with pleasure.

"I don't know what to think." He rubbed his chin as if trying to solve a mystery. "This is a surprising invitation from you, a girl who thinks romance is ridiculous. I thought this wedding was the worst thing to happen in your life."

"Recently I've learned there are worse things," Kelsey admitted, making a rueful face. "I discovered that losing a friend can be more painful than even a trip to the dentist. You know, romance should be one step past friendship." Acting braver than she felt, she reached for his hand and laced her fingers through his.

"I see what you mean. If you don't mind, I have one more question before I tell you whether or not I'll go to the wedding."

Just when she thought she had it made, he was looking for excuses to turn her down! Kelsey's heart ached. She had known getting Shawn back was a risky proposition, and now it looked as though she had gambled and lost. She supposed it was better to have tried and failed than to end up wondering for the rest of the year what could have happened. But somehow she didn't feel consoled.

She tried to pull her hand back, but Shawn only gripped it more tightly. He cleared his throat, and she noticed the telltale sparkle in his eyes. She heaved a sigh of relief. Everything was going to be all right.

"I was wondering if you're inviting me as a friend." He held his breath, waiting for her answer.

Was that all he wanted to know? She knew Patty would have some cute answer, but the truth was all Kelsey needed. She smiled, and he smiled back. "We've been friends for a while now, Shawn. I think it's time for us to be more than friends."